ARROWS
AND
SNAKESKIN

D1225391

Sidney N. Riggs

ARROWS
AND
SNAKESKIN

J. B. LIPPINCOTT COMPANY

Philadelphia and New York

CLEAVELAND HOUSE BOOKS
FACSIMILE EDITION
WEST TISBURY, MASS.

FACSIMILE EDITION PUBLISHED BY

CLEAVELAND HOUSE BOOKS, WEST TISBURY, MASS.

COPYRIGHT 2010

ISBN 978-0-9844446-0-1

ORIGINALLY PUBLISHED

BY J.B. LIPPINCOTT COMPANY,

PHILADELPHIA AND NEW YORK

COPYRIGHT 1962 BY SIDNEY N. RIGGS

LIBRARY OF CONGRESS CATALOG CARD NO. 62-9327

JACKET ART BY DONALD BOLOGNESE

"The great people of the Narragansetts, in a braving manner, sente a messenger unto them with a bundl of arrows tyed aboute with a great sneak-skine; which their interpretours tould them was a threatening & a challeng. Upon which the Gov'r, with the advice of others, sente them a round an-swere, that if they had rather have warre than peace, they might begine when they would; they had done them no wrong, neither did they fear them, or should they find them unprovided. And by another messenger sent the sneake-skine back with bulits in it; but they would not receive it, but sent it back againe."

Of Plimoth Plantation
WILLIAM BRADFORD

CONTENTS

Cast of Characters   9

Chapter One   THE CAPTIVE   11

Chapter Two   CHEEGUT   32

Chapter Three   KISWIS STRIKES   44

Chapter Four   PLANS TO ESCAPE   54

Chapter Five   THE FLIGHT   62

Chapter Six   THE TALKING LEAVES   76

Chapter Seven   A FIRE IS KINDLED   83

Chapter Eight   OUTLAWS   101

Chapter Nine   THE RAID   125

Chapter Ten   WAR!   137

Chapter Eleven   THE ENGLISH STRIKE   154

Chapter Twelve   DEATH OF A NATION   164

Chapter Thirteen   END OF THE TRAIL   178

Glossary of Pequot Indian Words   189

CAST OF CHARACTERS

The main characters in this story are:

John Bishop — A fourteen-year-old "bound boy" who is kidnaped by a Pequot raiding party led by

Kithansh — a brother of the Pequot king,

Sassacus — who hates all white people because his father was murdered at a Dutch trading post.

Wegun — a former Narragansett princess, is the wife of

Mononotto — a Pequot sachem second only to the king. His only surviving son is an eight-year-old,

Nemud — who tries to be everything that John is.

Kiswis — hates everybody, especially John. He dies a shameful death, but is a hero to the Pequots.

Mommenoteck — is an aged sachem of the Pequotoog who was once kidnaped by the English and learned their language and their strength.

Roger Williams — the white father of the Narragansetts, offers to help John, but the aid is too late.

Susan and Hepsy Swain — are two girls who are able to repay a debt to John and Wegun's family, through the agency of

John Winthrop — the governor of the Colony of the Massachusetts Bay.

A host of characters, minor to this story, but many of them famous in New England history, are to be found influencing or threatening John's life. They are of the strong tribes of Indians and the English colonial troops.

Chapter One

THE CAPTIVE

JOHN stopped to listen. There was a rustling of dry oak leaves and then all was still. He crouched behind a clump of junipers and peered through the branches toward the thicket that covered the hill above him.

There was no sign of the cow or of any other living thing and yet there had been that tiny sound.

Previously when Daisy had broken out of her pen, John had been able to find her by the trail of broken branches and by the noise she had made. This sound was not like that. It was just a whisper in the leaves as if something was trying to be quiet.

A chilly wind stirred the dead grass. In the runlets, leading down to the Connecticut River, spring had unlocked the waters, leaving thin films of ice against the banks. Across the river, the sun peeped over the treetops. Wisps of mist rose from the water.

It had been dark when he was roused from his bed on the floor of the loft. He had just started his chores when Master Hoskins discovered the broken pen. Daisy had pushed her way out during the night.

"Go find that cow!" he had shouted. "Don't come back until you get her. I've been clothing and feeding you for nigh on eight years and now you've paid me back by letting the cow escape!"

John was still hurt by this accusation. Ever since he was six, when his mother had died, he had worked hard. It was bad enough to be an orphan without having his guardian accuse him of carelessness.

He stepped out into the biting wind and looked down the broad valley. There didn't seem to be any sign of life. Then, without warning, there was a rush of feet and rough hands seized his arms. A wiry wrist cut into his throat. He gasped and struggled to breathe.

He remembered the wrestling holds his guardian had taught him. With a twist he broke away and turned to grapple with his attackers.

There were three of them, young Indians not more than three or four years older than he. Each one had his head shaved, with the exception of a bristly crest running from the forehead to a scalp-lock at the back. The hair was plastered with dried paint and decorated with beads and feathers. John smelled the odor of rancid grease that glistened on their bodies.

They closed in slowly on three sides as John watched them and became more tense. He could see that they were not like the Indians near Wethersfield, who were short and heavy. These braves were taller and their bodies looked trim and hard. *They must be Pequots!* he thought. *How can I get out of this?* He tried to back away, but the prickly evergreen branches held him fast.

The tallest Indian, the one who had tried to choke him, scowled and crouched as he moved in to attack once more. John watched his chance and gripped the young brave's arm for a wrestling hold. His hands slipped on the greased skin. He grabbed for another hold. Then all three leaped at him and threw him to the ground.

He filled his lungs to shout. The leader raised his war club and John tried to dodge but the weapon hit the back of his head with the sound of a deep-toned bell and he knew no more.

The sun was well above the treetops when he awoke to a confused world of pain and strange sounds. His head throbbed. He longed for some of the water that he seemed to hear gurgling near his ear. Then he realized that his arms were bound behind him and that he was lying on his side. When he tried to move his legs, he found that they were also tied. Legs and arms were stiff and numb. He opened his eyes for an instant and then closed them as the pain shot through his head.

He was soon aware that he was in a boat. The sounds he had heard were the rhythmical beats of the paddles and the rush of water past the hull. He opened his eyes again and saw, in front of him, three Indians swinging their slim paddles and dipping in unison. The one who seemed to be their leader was kneeling in the center among the skin-covered packs and pouches. John could hear other paddlers behind him. He struggled to sit up, and there was a change in the rhythm.

The leader watched him for a moment, then signaled to the Indian back of John. The brave stopped and laid his paddle across the thwarts, and John twisted his head to catch a few drops of water in his mouth as they fell on him from the wet blade.

The brave untied the rawhide thongs that had bound

13

him. John could feel the blood burning its way into his numb hands and feet. They were the same pains he felt when he had worked too long in the snow and then warmed himself in the fireplace heat.

The leader signaled to him with two motions: a finger on his lips to be quiet, and a downward stroke with his fist showing he would be beaten. John nodded. Five against one was too much to fight against.

When he was able to sit up he could see that they were paddling on the main part of the Connecticut River. The current flowed with them and green rushes along the bank nodded gracefully. Trees on the hillside were covered with a haze of pink and green as buds struggled to burst into leaf and bloom.

John reached over the side to get water in his hand. Then he stopped as he saw a gourd dipper near the leader's feet. He motioned toward it. The young brave shook his head and indicated that he was to dip with his hand.

"Much *nuppe*—bad," he said, motioning toward the gourd. "You—" and he scooped once more with his hand.

The water was good. Each handful of drops helped to soften his parched mouth. When his thirst was satisfied he said to the leader, "Do you speak English?"

The young man stopped paddling and nodded. *"Biangut,"* he said. Then, seeing John's questioning look, he pointed to the woven blanket that was rolled up with the other packs.

"Blanket?" said John.

"Yes—biangut. Him English biangut." Then he added in a loud voice, *"Debe."*

There was a stir among the other Indians. Those John

could see shook their heads, and one of them pointed ahead, down the river.

"*Machemoodus—cheephuggey Hobbamuck!*" he said with tight lips. Then he dug in deeper and harder with his paddle.

"Him *wenai,*" the leader said. He made a motion as if he were hobbling with a cane and added, "Woman. Him afraid of Evil One at Machemoodus."

I must learn enough of their language to help me escape. They don't seem cruel now, but they may be saving me for torture. He tried to think of a plan to get away before it was too late. He shuddered when he remembered the stories of Indian treatment of captive white people.

Now he began to feel the effects of sitting up. He was dizzy and he felt sick, so he lay down on the bottom of the canoe. The warm sun and the easy motion of the craft made him drowsy, and soon he was asleep.

The sun was low in the west when John awakened. He struggled to sit up and felt that every bone and muscle was aching. He could see that the river was now much wider and straighter. The approach of evening seemed to bring a feeling of danger. Then he saw that the Indians were tense and silent. It looked as if they expected an attack. They watched the left bank of the river as the cadence of their paddles increased.

They approached the mouth of a wide stream that flowed down from the north. A narrow point separated it from the river and dwindled to a sand bar with a few stones and rushes. Now they were opposite the stream, and still John could see no cause for fear.

Then he heard it. There was a deep, rumbling groan,

more to be felt than heard. The hairs on the back of his neck stiffened and he could feel a chill along his spine. His captors moaned and their paddle strokes became irregular. John could see that the young Indians were frightened. Even the leader no longer looked confident. He worked as hard as the others to get the canoe away from that place.

John wished he could take a paddle and help. Instead, he had to sit still in fear. This must be Machemoodus, where he had heard the leader say the evil one lived.

He could do nothing to help get away, so he found himself praying. Suddenly he realized that he was not in a blind panic. The Indians splashed with their paddles, and nearly tumbled out of the canoe in their haste to escape, but he no longer feared. With this comfort came an idea.

If I can get away from them tonight, I'll come back here to hide until they are gone. The Indians will be afraid to go near that hill. There must be a good reason for all that noise and I'm not going to fear it, even if the Indians do.

As the rumble and groan of Machemoodus grew fainter, the braves' spirits seemed to rise. They were now stroking in cadence and breathing more regularly. One of the paddlers grunted and motioned toward the leader. *"Wenai! Huh!"* he said. All of them laughed except the leader. He set his jaw and stared straight ahead.

It was almost nightfall when the leader signaled to the paddlers and they swung the canoe to the right bank. They stepped ashore on the dry grass, carrying their packs. One of them tossed John the woolen blanket. They hid the dugout in the mouth of a small brook and covered it with branches. Their leader looked at the hiding place, smoothed out a faint footprint in the grass, and nodded.

In making preparations for the night each Indian placed his pack where it would cause the least disturbance to the grass and brush. Then he unrolled it. They lit no fire but dipped into their pouches for dried food. They squatted in a circle, chewing slowly. Then they washed the food down with sips of water from a gourd that they passed around the circle.

The leader handed John his portion and called it by its Indian name. "This *yokeg*," he said as he put parched corn in his outstretched hand. "This *quahaug*," he added as he stripped from a slender twig several objects that looked like dried apples.

The corn was tender and crunchy. Prudence Hoskins had roasted corn like this in the long-handled skillet over the fireplace coals. The dried object puzzled him until he had chewed on it for a while. When he began to get taste from it, he recognized it as a hard-shelled clam, the kind the fishermen raked from the sandy coves and brought to Watertown to peddle. Now he remembered that name they used to distinguish these from the long-necked, soft-shelled clams that spat jets of water from the sand flats.

Preparation for sleep was also simple. The leader un-rolled the woolen blanket and motioned John to use it. The others curled up in their soft deerskins and were soon asleep. One Indian sat up to watch. He pulled his deer-skin around his shoulders and looked out toward the river.

John said, "Machemoodus?" The leader shook his head, "Wangunks." He spat on the ground. "Him come like *shkook* in night." He wriggled his hand through the grass as he repeated, "Shkook."

17

John could hear the breathing of the Indians and he pretended that he too was asleep. *Now is my only chance. If I can slip away, without the sentry knowing it, I can get back to the hill. I'll have to swim the river, but they won't dare follow.*

He lumped up his blanket and slid cautiously toward a gap in the circle of sleeping braves. Only a few miles and he'd be in the shelter of the hill. One of the Indians stirred and John held his breath. Then he inched along, making his aching muscles drag him to the safety of the thicket.

When he got into the thick brush he removed his cowhide shoes and tied them about his neck by the laces. As he looked back he could see the guard still facing toward the river.

John rose to his feet and started north along the river bank. His stockinged feet felt out the rough ground. Every stone and twig hurt, but anything seemed better than captivity and torture. Now that he was a distance from the camp, he moved more swiftly, keeping watch of the river so that he would not lose his way.

He had gone a good distance and now felt better. Soon he would be able to see the sandy point across the river and swim to safety. Then he heard a slight noise directly ahead of him. *Wangunks*, he thought. *They're not as bad as the Pequots, but I don't want to meet any Indians now.* He stopped near a large tree and looked about. There was a slight movement in the thicker woods away from the river. Then a twig snapped behind him and he turned in time to dodge a blow from a war club.

"Come," said the leader, "you do bad thing."

John thought for a moment of dashing toward the river, but saw that he was surrounded. All of the aches and pains seemed redoubled as his captors dragged him back to the sleeping place. This time the leader bound his hands and feet with rawhide and threw him on his blanket. He could hear the braves grumble as they curled up to continue their interrupted sleep.

He struggled, quietly, to get rid of his bonds, but the tough hide would not slip loose. Finally he fell into a sleep of exhaustion, broken by nightmares of escape and recapture repeated over and over.

John awoke when a rough hand grabbed his shoulder. He tried to sit up but found that he could not move. The leader came to him and untied the tough hide strips. He ached all over and his head wound throbbed with dull pain.

He expected rough treatment because of his attempt to escape, but the Indians seemed to ignore him. *If I'm to be tortured or made a slave they wouldn't act this way. What do they plan to do with me?*

The braves rolled their packs and brushed out the matted places in the dry grass. Breakfast was the same as the evening meal: yokeg and quahaugs washed down with brook water. While they were eating, the leader pointed his thumb toward his chest and said, "Me, Kithansh," then, pointing to John, he asked, "You?"

"My name is John Bishop."

Kithansh was silent for a moment as he moved his lips on the unfamiliar sound. Then he shook his head and said, "You—John."

He turned to the other Indians and spoke to them. One after another told his name and showed it in sign language.

"Tulepas," one of them said. Then he drew a rough picture in the sand. John recognized a turtle before the brave rubbed it out with his hand.

"Wahsus," said another, and he lurched about as a bear.

"Me, Teecommewas!" said another as he stood at a crouch and struck downward with one clenched fist after the other.

"They all teecommewas," Kithansh said. "Mother, brother, all same. All strikers."

Wunx was a friendly Indian. His name, fox, did not seem appropriate. He had widely spaced eyes and a straight-forward gaze. It was Kiswis who looked the part of the fox, and a very mean one. During the introductions he pretended to work on his pack, occasionally glaring at the white boy through half-closed eyes. When Kithansh spoke his name, Kiswis turned his back to them.

When they start the torture that will be the one to do the worst, John thought.

The sun was just rising when they pushed the dugout from its hiding place, brushed out traces of having been there, and paddled out into the river. John noticed that it was Wunx who made the final check.

John envied the Indians their task of paddling. They kept warm while he shivered in the chill of the early-morning mist. He huddled in the bottom of the canoe but made no attempt to reach for the blanket. *I won't let them think that a white boy cannot stand the cold.*

The sun was high when they came to the widest part of the river. There were low sandy shores and shoals that would force larger craft out in the channel. The Pequots kept so far over to the eastern shore that their paddles grated on the bottom. John felt that he could almost reach out and touch the beach grass.

He looked across the wide river mouth and saw a fort on a sandy point. The palisade was made of stout logs driven into the ground and set close together. They were sharpened at the tops. There were narrow openings through which muzzles of bronze cannon could be seen. *That must be Fort Saybrook,* John thought. *I've heard people talk about the English fort at the mouth of the Connecticut River. I wonder if they will see me and send help.* He sat up straighter so anyone who watched would know he was white.

"They *wonnux,*" Kithansh said as he pointed toward the fort. "You wonnux—they wonnux."

The Indians were now paddling faster as they glanced sidewise toward the distant fort. John motioned in that direction and said, "Do you fear wonnux—like debe?"

Kithansh waved his hand violently from side to side, "No Pequot fear wonnux. Pequot fear *bushkeagun.* Bushkeag go 'boom.' Bushkeag kill far off."

As they left the fort behind them, John despaired of escape or rescue. No white man had shown himself, and the guns had been silent.

The waves of Long Island Sound broke over the shoals, rocking the canoe so that John grabbed the gunwales. Cold spray dashed over him. He could taste salt on his lips. The paddlers dipped steadily without seeming to notice the rough water. Soon he was able to balance himself to the roll of the light craft.

That afternoon they passed the mouth of a broad river, almost as wide as the Connecticut. Later, as the sun seemed to be dipping into the water behind them, they turned into a harbor and pulled toward a sandy beach.

John saw a fort on top of a low hill that rose several hundred paces from the shore. Several Indians stood on the beach looking in their direction. Others were streaming out of the entrance and running toward them. By the time the dugout had grated on the sand a crowd of men, women, children, and dogs had gathered. Others were still coming from the fort. The shrill voices of the squaws and children mingled with the barking and snarling of the dogs. Several dogfights added to the confusion.

Kithansh motioned to him to get out and wade ashore with them. He took off his shoes and stepped into the cold water. When he reached dry land he found himself in the center of a screaming crowd of squaws who struck at him with fists and sticks. The curs snapped at his bare legs. He stumbled and nearly fell. He was dizzy and his wounded head throbbed.

Kithansh pushed his way through the crowd, sending several of John's attackers sprawling. He grasped the arm of an old crone who had raised a hawklike hand to rake the boy's face, and pushed her aside. Then he placed one arm about John's shoulders and, raising his other hand, he shouted, *"Nichie Sassacus!"*

The noise and confusion stopped as if by magic. The crowd moved back, stumbling over each other. Squaws herded their children away and beat the dogs with their sticks.

When all was still the young brave started to speak. His voice was firm as he talked in the language of the Pequots. John got the impression that these people had now recognized Kithansh and that he must be an important person. *Those words "Nichie Sassacus" must have some meaning to make them stop as they did. They acted as if they were afraid.* He looked at the quiet crowd and felt Kithansh's arm about him. *I'm being protected,* he thought, *but why?*

Kithansh talked and gestured, sometimes pointing toward the white boy and saying, *"Wegun muckachuck."* He repeated *"Mononotto"* several times. Each time he said it he clenched his fist. The squaws looked subdued. They were no longer ready to scream and claw. Their broad faces smoothed out, and a few of them nodded at the word Wegun.

When Kithansh finished, he waved toward the fort. Without a word the crowd turned and trudged up toward the gateway, leaving the small party on the shore. One squaw turned and raised her hand toward John in a timid sign of greeting.

Kithansh motioned to his companions to draw the canoe high up on the shore. Then they shouldered their packs and walked toward the palisaded fort. John held his head high. "Whatever they do to me, I'll face it like a white boy," he murmured.

The fort was a large circle of slender logs driven into the earth and sharpened at the top. They were spaced like pickets in a fence, with openings too narrow for even a child to slip through. The entrance was formed by one part of the circle overlapping the other. John could not see directly into the enclosure.

When they were inside, he could see crowded huts, resembling the beehives at Wethersfield. They were arranged in narrow streets that ran from north to south.

An old Indian greeted Kithansh. He shrugged and spread his hands as if to apologize for the actions of the villagers. He led them to a hut that was set apart from the others.

It was large and dome-shaped. The roof, covered with a heavy thatch of grass and reeds, sloped down like eaves over the bark walls. A thin curl of smoke rose from a hole at the top.

When they entered the doorway, John stopped to see where he was going. Smoke from the fire, which smoldered on a circular hearth in the center, filled the hut and brought tears to his eyes. A thin beam of light found its way through the hole in the roof. When the fire flared up he could see a squaw bending over, arranging cooking pots and bowls of food.

The floor was beaten earth. Around the walls stood low benches or beds. They were made of poles lashed to stout, forked sticks that were driven into the ground. These frames were covered with straight branches, dried rushes, and sleeping mats. A few had tanned deerskins thrown over them.

Kithansh and the young braves put their packs on the beds, then squatted about the fire with their feet flat on the floor. John tried to copy them but found that it cramped his legs. He felt dizzy, so he sat on the ground with his arms about his knees. He could see his captors staring into the fire, their eyes and bared teeth showing white against the dark of their faces.

The squaw stirred the mixture in the pot and then reached for a pile of dry, blackened objects that looked like chips. These she crumbled into the steaming mess and continued to stir. He caught the odor of long-dead fish. He wondered if he could eat this strange stew. He looked at the young braves and saw that they were leaning forward, sniffing and licking their lips.

The squaw dipped into the pot with a large wooden spoon and blew on the steaming mess until she could taste of it. She grunted and ladled out, into wooden bowls, a portion for each of them. She stuck a crude spoon in each of the bowls and passed them to the braves.

When she handed one to John, he held his head to one side to avoid the smell. He took a mouthful. It burned his tongue and he thought he was going to be sick. *Why did she have to spoil good succotash with that smelly fish?* He didn't dare put the food aside. *Maybe I can eat it if I hold my breath.*

It was hard to take. The stew was unsalted, but it was hot and it filled his stomach. Soon he no longer felt hungry but his head ached and his eyes burned with the sting of smoke and with weariness. He nodded and put his hands on the floor to steady himself.

Kithansh grasped his arm. *"Bedunk,"* he said, pointing to one of the platforms. "You sleep."

John sat on the edge of the bed and pulled off his shoes. He could feel the spring of the smooth branches and the softness of the rushes and sleeping mats. *This is better than my corn-husk pallet in the loft at the Hoskins' house.* He rolled up his coat for a pillow, pulled the blanket over him, and fell asleep before he could think of more plans for escape.

When John awakened he looked about him. For several minutes he couldn't straighten things out in his mind. All that he had been through seemed like a bad dream. He expected to see the rafters and thatch of his loft bedroom back at Wethersfield. Daisy should be safe in her rickety pen, and Prudence Hoskins be rattling pans in the fireplace down there in the living room at the foot of the ladder.

Then came the realization of the smells of Indian food and the sting of smoke in his eyes. The old squaw crouched at the cooking fire as if she had not moved since the night before. He sat up stiffly and reached for his shoes. He thought his head would burst. He was dizzy and fought off the feeling that he would be sick. Dressing was no problem. He laced his shoes, put on his waist belt, and he was dressed.

"*Weeqwasun,*" said Kithansh. Then he added, "*Geesh-tush,*" and went through the motions of washing himself. He led John outside where there was a birchbark pail, half full of water, and a large wooden bowl. John watched his captors and copied what they did. He chewed a twig from a dogwood tree until it was tufted at the end, and then cleaned his teeth. He reached for fine sand in a birchbark box to rub on his wet hands. When he put water on his head he winced with the pain. He felt gingerly for where he had been struck. There was a gash with a large swelling around it. His long hair was matted with dried blood.

The young braves scrubbed themselves carefully. When they finished they carried the bowl a distance from the lodge to empty it.

Breakfast was the same as the evening meal. This time

it tasted better. John ate his bowl of food and was about to ask for more, when he suddenly felt full.

After they had finished their meal, the five young braves rolled their packs and strode out without a backward look. Kithansh motioned to John and he followed.

They walked in single file with John placed second in the line, next to the leader. With four braves behind him, John knew that he had no chance to dash for freedom. The trail led from the sheltered harbor toward the rolling hills to the westward. They moved quickly, without the usual caution. In spite of their fast pace, John was keenly aware of the noise he was making as he stumbled along in his clumsy shoes.

They had not been traveling long when another Indian fort appeared ahead of them. As they neared the top of the hill on which this stockade stood, John looked back and saw the sparkle of the water in the harbor they had just left. In all directions the view was clear. Trees and underbrush had been removed so that no one could approach without being seen.

The logs in the palisade were tall, almost twice the height of Kithansh. They were sharpened at the top like those at the Mystic fort, and the entrance was closed by stiff brush with the branches pointing outward.

"Weinshauks," Kithansh said, pointing to the fort. "Sachem Sassacus, him here. Wegun, Mononotto, him here." He turned toward the gate and called, *"Aque!"*

There was no answer from the fort, but the barricade of branches moved out slowly. Several squaws staggered under the load of a single tree.

The party made no attempt to enter. The young braves

27

waited, staring at the entrance. Then a double file of warriors came out to form a lane reaching almost to where they stood. *This is the finish,* John thought. *It is the beginning of the torture I have heard about, where the prisoner has to run through while they strike with clubs.*

There was a stir and a tall warrior walked out of the gateway and came toward them through the files of braves. He wore a long cloak covered with feathers which overlapped to form a pattern of blue and red against a background of soft gray and brown. His cap was decorated with white and purple beads, and beneath the feathered cloak John could see an apron trimmed with what appeared to be embroidery.

He looked very much like Kithansh. He was tall and slim. His complexion was the same clear, light bronze color.

"Nichie!" he exclaimed, as he grasped Kithansh by both arms. Then he stood back and motioned toward John with his thumb and frowned. "Wonnux?" he spat out.

The young brave answered him, motioning toward the boy as he talked. The sachem stared at John, then he grunted a few words and turned to walk toward the entrance. Kithansh and his braves followed, taking John with them through the double rank of Indians. They stared at the boy and several of them fingered the weapons in their belts.

"Him Sassacus," Kithansh said. "Him big sachem for all Pequotoog. Me and him—nichie." He linked his fingers together to show a close relationship.

"Is he your friend?" John asked.

"Friend—*netop.* Him more—him *nichie.*"

I'm sure he's no friend of mine, John thought, *nor of anyone who is white.*

When they were inside the palisade, John saw an area almost as large as William Hoskins' four-acre farm that he had helped to clear of stumps and to till. He remembered how he had ached all over at the close of each day's labor. Now he felt worse. *I'll not give in. They are not going to think a white boy is a weakling.*

Dome-shaped lodges, with thatched roofs, formed an orderly circle. In the center was a space, cleared except for a strange pair of trees that were grown together several feet above the ground, forming a crude letter "H."

"*Guldooke,*" Kithansh said as he pointed to the trees. "Him—good—luck. We dance. We win fight."

Sassacus had gone on to a lodge more than twice the size of any of those in the circle. There were other large structures, and it was toward one of these that Kithansh led John.

Swarms of naked children played with colored pebbles in the dust in front of the lodges and in the dancing place. Some of the boys and girls were nearly as old as John. He tried to look away, but they seemed to be all about him.

Kithansh pointed toward the lodge. "Him—Mononotto. Squaw—him Wegun."

John followed him through the mass of children. He heard one cry out in pain, and he looked down. A little one was holding his foot and screaming.

"I'm sorry," John said as he kneeled to comfort the young one. "Why, you're only a baby and I must have stepped on your foot. There, don't cry any more."

The little fellow stopped crying to stare at this stranger.

29

Then he smiled, while tears were still running down his fat cheeks, and said something in Indian baby-talk.

"I did not mean to hurt him," John said, turning to Kithansh. He knew that he could not be understood, but he felt that he must say something. Then, to his relief, he saw that his actions had spoken for him. The Indians smiled and nodded their heads.

As he moved toward the doorway he saw a woman whose expression reminded him of his mother. *This must be Wegun,* he thought as he moved toward her.

Wegun was tall and slim. Her skin was lighter and smoother than that of other Indian women he had seen. Her black hair was drawn back from her forehead and woven into a thick braid that hung down her back. A small cap, ornamented with beads and scallop shells, looked like a jeweled coronet on her head.

She was dressed in a long, fringed skirt that reached to her ankles. A soft, deerskin shirt, ornamented with heavy embroidery of white beads and shells, fell over the skirt and was gathered around her slim waist with a beaded belt.

Wegun smiled and held out both hands to John. *"Ahu-panum muckachuck,"* she said in a low voice.

John almost staggered with weakness as he walked toward her. She placed both hands on his head. He winced as she touched the wound, and Wegun swung around to Kithansh with a quick question.

The young brave hung his head and scraped a spot in the dust with his moccasin. Then he spoke and seemed to explain how the boy had been wounded. He was not finished when Wegun turned to a basket filled with packets tied with thin sinews. She opened one and made a pad of the dried herbs. This she soaked in cold water and placed it gently on the wound. When she had fastened it in place she patted him on the shoulder and led him into the lodge.

John didn't know whether it was the dressing of the wound or Wegun's kindness that did it, but his head felt better almost at once.

Wegun spread an armload of dry rushes on a bed platform near the door of the lodge and covered it with sleeping mats and a deerskin. Then she motioned to John that he was to lie down.

He took off his heavy shoes and stretched out on the springy bed. Wegun covered him with a woven blanket and put her fingers on his eyelids to close them.

This is not what I expected, but I must get back to Wethersfield, no matter how kind some of them are, John thought. He remembered what his mother had said just before she had died, "John, Governor Winthrop will bind you to some good man, as you will be an orphan. It is your duty to obey him and to work for him, as if he were your own father. When you are a man you will be free to do as you wish."

Then he slept.

Chapter Two

CHEEGUT

JOHN awoke from a feverish dream. He seemed to be trying over and over again to do something that had to be done. He knew there must be a desperate need for action, but didn't know what it was.

Then he felt Wegun's cool fingers on his forehead, and she raised his head to let him sip water from a gourd dipper.

He slept, and awoke each time fresh dressings were placed on his wound. And each time Wegun put her arm about his shoulders to raise him and held a gourd to his lips. The drink was hot and aromatic. It smelled like the remedy that Mistress Hoskins used for fevers and nearly every ache and pain. *It must be boneset,* John thought. He nearly gagged on it. Then he slept, and when he awoke he felt better. Bad dreams were a thing of the past. What had been troubling him was his duty to get back to Wethersfield.

He looked about him from the low bed near the doorway. He could not see outside because of a large mat that hung there and extended into the room. There was another mat across the room on the other side of the entrance. This protected two bedsteads.

He raised his head and felt no pain. There was a stir

from a bed next to his and he saw a small Indian boy sitting cross-legged on the mat. John thought he must be seven or eight years old. His bright eyes glistened in the light from the fire. He seemed eager to speak as he leaned forward.

"Aque," said John, and made a motion of greeting with his hand.

The boy sat up suddenly and then began to chatter in his language.

John didn't know what he was trying to say, but it sounded friendly. Then there was movement back of the mats to the rear of the lodge and Wegun pushed aside the deerskin curtain. She came in and hushed the boy. John heard her call him Nemud. Then she kneeled beside John's bed and felt of his forehead. She nodded and pulled the blanket around his neck.

During the next few days John felt that he was growing stronger. He could sit up without the pounding pain in his head. He felt hungry for more than the broth and gruel. He liked the mixture of corn meal cooked with dried berries, especially when the squaw who worked for Wegun sweetened it with wild honey. He wanted solid food. Above all he wanted to get outside in the sunshine.

When he tried to go to the door, early in his recovery, he staggered, and Wegun had put him back to bed. She frowned and motioned that he was to stay there.

Each day she sat beside him and taught him to speak Pequot. He found that he must listen for small differences in sounds.

"Makia wis," she said, and pointed first to the boy and then held her hand close to the floor.

That must mean small boy, John thought. He turned to Nemud and said, *"Makawis."* The boy rolled over on the bed platform, laughing so hard that tears trickled down his cheeks. Then he sat up and flapped his arms like wings.

Wegun seemed amused. "Makia wis—Muckachuck," and she signaled for small. "Makawis—" She paused a moment, and then gave the call that John recognized as that of the whippoorwill.

There were many times that Nemud was amused at John's mistakes until the Indian started to learn English, then the white boy had his chance to laugh.

John had noticed a tall brave who came in and out of the lodge without glancing in his direction. He was heavier than Kithansh and carried himself proudly. He did not smile, yet John felt there was goodness about him. *If this is Mononotto,* he thought, *why did Kithansh double his fist when he mentioned his name there at the harbor fort? Perhaps it is because Mononotto has the power to punish.*

Then he heard Wegun and Mononotto freely talking in their mat-screened room, and he realized they did so because he could not understand what they were saying. The brave mentioned *"muckachuck"* several times, as if asking questions.

When Mononotto passed through, he walked over to John and said, "Aque, muckachuck," then he left before John could answer.

The rear of the lodge was screened from the front by large mats that hung from a pole stretching across the center. Openings were left on either side of the hearth to serve as doorways. These were draped with curtains of deerskin that fell in soft folds.

34

A pile of mats, covered with a thickly furred hide, was back of the fireplace, facing the door of the lodge. Here he saw Mononotto and Wegun at mealtimes, when the old squaw served them from the cooking pots.

John was soon able to go for short walks outside the lodge. The air felt soft with the warmth of late spring. Leaves were turning a darker green. He could see squaws digging in the gardens outside the palisade. They stooped and hacked away with their short hoes made of crooked sticks.

Braves strode past him and stared, then looked away. Groups of squaws stopped talking for a moment as they watched him. Then they continued their gabbling, and John was sure they were talking about him and wondering.

They can't be wondering any more than I am, he thought.

As the days grew warm and sunny John became restless. He felt strong enough to run and jump. In the past springs, he had been laboring in the fields with William Hoskins. It would be good to work again.

A group of squaws walked toward the gate carrying short-handled Indian hoes. John picked up one of the crooked sticks and started to go with them. The squaws drew away from him, and one old woman snatched the hoe from his hand and pushed him off. She rejoined the others and they filed out of the gate, talking to each other and looking back at him. An old brave, standing nearby, moved his hand with upraised thumb in the Indian sign of disapproval.

John returned to the lodge and watched Wegun weave baskets. She formed a frame of peeled willow branches.

Then she twisted dried rushes in and out until the basket seemed to grow of its own accord. She patted a place on the mat beside her.

He sat down to watch. Then he picked up pieces of willow to shape a frame like hers, but she took them from him. She made the sign of disapproval. "Weaving—planting—squaw work," she said. John got to his feet and wandered out into the sunlight.

Off in the distance he could hear the whoops of boys. Through the cracks between the upright logs of the palisade he could see them playing on the bank of the stream that flowed at the foot of the hill.

He watched them for a while, then he turned away and tried to find something to do. He was watching a tiny stream of ants, carrying their burdens to their hill, when an old brave came to him and put his hand on his shoulder. "Come," he said, "Wegun send."

John walked with him toward the gateway. A young brave stepped out to bar his way, but the old man spoke to him and the sentry stood aside. His guide gave him a rough push and pointed toward the boys. Before John could thank him the brave had turned and stalked away.

John walked down the hill to the stream. The clear water ran slowly over the sand and pebble bottom. The boys were playing a game in which they raced after one another and slapped bare backs with the palms of their hands. They dodged and shouted as they whacked each other. He stood there for a moment and shook his head.

Then the boys looked toward him and suddenly the game stopped. Now he could hear the sound of birds in the bushes across the water. The boys walked off a short distance and sat down in a group to talk. He knew that they were speaking about him, because he could see them look in his direction.

John took off his shoes and dipped his feet in the water. It was cold, but it felt good. Then he removed his shirt to let the warmth of the sun soak into his skin. This was the time of year that Master Hoskins occasionally relaxed enough to show him how to swim and wrestle. It felt good, at the end of a hard day's work in the field to find new use for his muscles. The water of the Connecticut River seemed to wash away the aches along with the soil of the farm. His guardian became sullen after each of these sessions, as if he felt he had sinned in getting any pleasure from sports.

When John stripped off his clothes he heard the boys exclaim. His white skin made him feel very naked. He could hear a movement behind him as if some of them were hiding in the bushes.

A thick branch of a fallen tree jutted out over the stream. John picked up a stick to probe for bottom and tossed it ashore when he found out how deep the stream was. He bounced several times on the springy limb, and then flashed into a clean dive that hardly stirred the water. He came to the surface, gasping for breath, and struck out with a strong overhand stroke for the opposite bank.

The hot sun warmed him. A few minutes later he dived in again with a shallow plunge. It did not seem so cold this time as he swam down the stream with the current. He surface-dived, to find that the stream was clear and deep. When he came to the top he flung the water from his long hair with a jerk of his head. When the cold struck deep into his body he came out and swished off the drops with his hands.

Several of the Indian lads came toward him from the alders, where they had hidden to watch. They walked over slowly and put their warm hands on his cool skin. One of them put his brown arm beside John's white one and shook his head.

"Duksors," he said, pointing his thumb to his brown chest. "You—John?"

He was nearly as tall as the white boy. His black eyes twinkled from beneath a mop of coarse black hair.

One boy motioned toward the water and pretended to shiver. Several others joined the group until there were about a dozen. Then John saw Nemud. He was the only small boy in the group. The others were about John's age. They talked among themselves, then they began to push each other toward the stream.

Duksors stripped off his breechcloth and ran out on the branch as he had seen John do. After a brief pause he jumped in with a great splash, landing flat on his stomach. He came up, gasping for breath, and swam for the shore with short underwater strokes. His friends whooped and followed him into the water, one after another, splashing from the limb and climbing out on the bank to get warm once more.

John dived in again, cutting the water cleanly. When he swam ashore the boys motioned that they wanted him to teach them. Duksors and a plump boy named Bopoose learned rapidly. When they raced, John found these two to be the only ones who could come close to finishing with him.

Nemud wanted to troop out on the branch for a dive, but John led him to a place where the bank was low over a shallow pool. There he taught him to go in head first.

When they tired of this play they sat in the sun to dry. They laughed when John spoke the few words in Pequot, but they rolled on the ground when Duksors and Bopoose tried English.

On their way back to the village they crowded about John trying to talk. Nemud grasped his hand and walked in step with him.

John held his head high and grinned. It was good to be alive and well. A dozen boys about his own age was more happiness than he had ever known. For the first time the thought of escape was dim.

Wegun heard the excited chatter and came to the door of the lodge. She nodded to John and looked toward the boys, who were all trying to talk at once. Nemud went to her and she put her arm around him, signaling to the others with her fingers on her lips.

Nemud stuttered and wriggled about. Finally he broke away to explain what had happened. He made diving and swimming motions, pointing to John as he spoke. The other boys nodded and added words to help the boy explain. When he finished, Wegun walked over to John and put her hand on his shoulder.

"*Kedeliwizi* Cheegut," she said.

The boys jumped up and down about John and shouted, "Cheegut, Cheegut." He knew he had been given an Indian name, but he did not know what it meant. It was probably good, because Wegun had given it to him.

Several days later, when John was about to join the boys

at the swimming place, he cupped a bit of bear grease in his hand and rubbed it into his skin. The sun had browned him until he looked almost as dark as his companions. He had found that his English clothes and heavy shoes were gone, and in their place were the summer clothes of a Pequot. He was pleased with the light moccasins and with the deerskin leggings that tied to his belt. The fringed shirt was especially soft and smelled strongly of the smoke in which the skin had been tanned. Now with the leggings he could go through brush and blackberry tangles without coming out with bleeding legs. The shirt would be fine for cool nights and rainy weather.

He was starting out to join the boys, when he met Kithansh. The young brave put out his hand to stop him. "Come," he said, and led John to where an old Indian sat, cross-legged, on a mat in front of one of the big lodges. He had a blanket draped over his shoulders and he seemed to doze in the warm sun.

A network of wrinkles covered his thin face. His high cheekbones stood out above his sunken cheeks. There were scars on his chest and arms where wounds had healed, leaving pink and brown patches. Kithansh stopped in front of the old man and said to John, "This Mommenoteck. Him old sachem, very wise."

The old Indian opened his eyes and blinked at the sunlight. He moistened his dry lips with his black tongue, then he looked at John and said, "Aque."

Kithansh spoke rapidly in Pequot and the old sachem sat up straighter. The young brave walked away, leaving the two of them together. Mommenoteck motioned to a place beside him. John squatted on the ground.

"The young sachem tells me you would know more about the Pequotoog," he said.

John stared at him. "You speak English very well," he said.

"More than three times ten summers ago, when I was in the land of the white man across the great water, I spoke it better. I taught Kithansh some English. He was too impatient to learn it well. Always in a hurry."

"I didn't know that any red men had ever been to England," John said.

"There have been many who have gone with the white men, most of them to their sorrow. Long ago I visited with our neighbors, the Wampanoags. A great canoe with wings sailed into their harbor. Five, four Wampanoags and myself, went out in a bark canoe to see this wonder. The bearded white men showed us many things. When we were in their lodge down inside, they spread the wings without our knowing it. When we felt the motion and heard the water rush by we were too far out to swim to the shore. We lived in this great canoe for more than two moons. We were often sick. We ate strange food. We began to learn the white man's tongue. Then we found ourselves at a place the whites call 'Plymouth.'"

The sachem paused, and John thought he had gone to sleep. He was about to get up when the old man opened his eyes and continued.

"The white people were kind. They taught us to speak the tongue of the English. They showed us many wonders. The whites were as the leaves in the forest. Their king wore a crown of yellow metal. He had a great army of *sanops*—more than I could count. They wore shining coats and carried the guns which we call 'bushkeagun.' Many of them carried long knives, which they called 'swords.' "

He was silent for a moment.

"I have told my people that the English are more fit to be called Pequotoog than the sanops of our nation. *Pequotoog* means 'Destroyers,' and the English can destroy more quickly than our red men.

"Our people have been named Pequotoog and they are proud to have others fear them. Our young sanops think that no one can beat us. They do not know what I know. They will not listen to an old man. They think they can kill or drive away all white people. It would be as easy to brush back the waves of the great water."

"There have been many Pequots who have been kind to me," John said. "Wegun and Kithansh have been my friends. Mononotto does not speak often but he is friendly."

"Yes, these are kind. They are of royal blood. But our king suffers from madness. He would kill all whites because his father was murdered by the whites called 'Dutch.' "

"Are there kings and nobles as in England?" John asked.

"There are, but not as in England. Among our nations the mother must be royal if the son is to rule. Nemud has royal blood from both parents. Wegun is a princess of the Narragansetts and Mononotto a Pequot prince, second only to Sassacus.

"Then we have the nobles and the warriors, who are called 'sanops.' They may own property and have the right to speak in council. The 'strangers' are those who come from other tribes. Those we capture become slaves. Some strangers come because they wish and they are free, but none may own property or have the right to speak in council.

"Now I am weary, Cheegut. Come to me when you are troubled."

"There is one thing I'd like to know," John said as he stood up to leave. "What is the meaning of the name 'Cheegut?'"

"It is a good title to give to a boy," replied the sachem. "Cheegut is the noble sea trout. He is the king of swimmers. Kithansh tells me you are well named." The old man settled back against the wall of the lodge and closed his eyes.

Chapter Three

KISWIS STRIKES

"W<small>HY</small> are you so silent, Cheegut?" Wegun asked. John looked up quickly. "I was thinking about my foster parents in Wethersfield. I wonder how they are."

"Foster parents?" Wegun turned to him. "What are they?"

"When my mother and father died, six years ago, Governor Winthrop bound me over to William and Prudence Hoskins, who then lived in the Massachusetts Bay Colony. They were to care for me as if I were their son. I was to work for them until I became a man."

"Were they kind to you, Cheegut?"

"They were not unkind. I worked hard and did as they told me."

"Did you have other white boys to play with?" Wegun put her hands on his shoulders and turned him toward her.

"There were no boys who lived near us. I didn't have much time for play after I had finished my work on the farm and around the cabin."

"It was not good. It is the play of the boy that strengthens him for his life as a man. You must spend more time with our boys. Learn the ways of the woods and of the red man." She pushed him toward the door of the lodge.

A group of the young Indians was standing nearby, waiting for him. The boys stopped talking among themselves as John approached. "Come with us tonight and hunt shore birds," said Duksors. "We drive them from their nests in the beach grass. You will be the hunter. You hold the basket and catch them as they run toward you."

"That sounds like good sport," John said. When he looked about him he could see several of the boys grin. Bopoose nudged another boy and winked.

"Yes, tonight, when all is dark, we go to the shore of the great sound. You will hold the basket and a torch. We beat the tall grass with sticks and shout as we move toward you. The stupid birds run toward the light and you catch them. You must be a good hunter."

While John was squatting at his evening meal, Wegun looked at him several times. Then she put her hand on his forehead.

"What troubles you?" she said. "Do you feel well?"

"I was just thinking. Tonight I am to go hunting with the boys for birds," he replied.

"Hunting? Hunting birds at night? Are you going to try to catch owls or whippoorwills?"

"No," John said. "We are to hunt the long-billed shore birds. I am the one to catch them as they drive the birds toward me. I don't want to fail—or get lost."

"And that is the reason you were worried?" Wegun went to the doorway and motioned for John to follow. "Come with me. You must learn how the red man finds his way in the dark when the sky is clear."

She smoothed a place in the dust with the palm of her hand. Then, with a stick, she marked a pattern of stars.

"This is Wahsus, the great bear. These stars, here and here and here, mark his body. Now remember this: two stars, like the lip of a drinking gourd, point to a bright star that marks the north. This north star never changes its place. Others are ever changing, but this one has marked the north as long as the red man can remember."

John nodded. "I'll remember."

"Look at the star before you start. Do not let the boys see you do it. Count your steps. When you make a turn, look for the star so you will know your new direction, then count. You cannot be lost if you count your steps in each direction, and think. A red man never stops thinking when he is on the trail."

As it grew dark the boys began to gather. Bopoose gave John a large basket, a net bag, and materials to make a torch. The long splinters of fat pine were lashed together with tough vines. Then he gave him a pair of shells of a big sea clam, tied shut, and a handful of soft fibers. The shell felt hot in his hands.

"This is your fire," Bopoose said. "It sleeps in a bed of dried punk and will glow when you open the shell and blow on it. The soft stuff is from the nest of the squirrel. This catches the fire and blazes up. Then you can light your torch from it."

"Come on," Duksors said. "It grows dark. The basket is big enough to catch a lot of birds." Some of the boys laughed.

As they left the village, John saw Kiswis standing near the gate with a twisted smile on his face. He wondered if the young sanop was up to some trick.

There was no moon. Stars clustered in the sky. In the

confused pattern he found the Great Bear. It was easy to see now, with its shape like a dipper. The two stars that formed the lip pointed straight to the bright North Star.

The little group walked in single file. They did not talk and each one stepped carefully to avoid making any sound. There was the North Star straight ahead. John counted his steps.

After a long walk they turned, and the star was now on his left. John started a new count, remembering how many paces he had gone toward the north. They waded a small stream and pushed their way through a swamp and a thick tangle of woods. In every clearing he looked for the friendly star.

At the next turn the star was behind them. *We must be going straight for the shore of the sound.*

They reached a belt of scrub pines and soft sand. There were goldenrod bushes and clumps of beach grass. The boys walked in zigzag patterns and made several large circles, but John was not confused. The star could not be changed.

"Here we stop," Duksors said. "Use the spark and the tinder to light your torch, then hold it in front of the open basket and wait. We'll spread out and drive the birds toward you. Do you understand?"

John understood better than they thought.

"When they run toward the fire and into the basket, grab them and wring their necks. When the net bag is full the hunt is over." The boys hurried off into the darkness.

As John waited he could hear the faint sound of waves washing upon the sandy shore to the south. He thought over the number of paces he had traveled in each direction

47

and figured that he must be almost opposite the Pequot harbor and the Mystic fort. Then he lit his torch.

The slivers of fat pine burned with a fragrant smell. Black smoke swirled about him and helped to keep away some of the mosquitoes. He thrust the end of the torch into the sand and put his other material in the basket. Then he headed west toward what he hoped would be Pequot harbor.

It was not long before he came to the shore. Across the still water he could see faint lights from the fort on the hill. He put his leggings and moccasins in the basket, lashed it to his head with the breechcloth, and waded into the cool salt water of the bay.

As he struck out, with the lights of the fort to guide him, he thought, *It's good to be away from those biting pests.*

When the shadows of the shore deepened, he reached for bottom and felt the sand beneath his feet. Then he waded out, climbed the low bank and put on his clothes. He shouldered the basket and set off at a trot for Weinshauks.

A sentry at the fort grabbed him as he passed near the gate. He looked in the basket and grunted, "Who are you?"

"I'm Cheegut. I go to Weinshauks."

"Yes. I know," said the sanop. "You come out of the water where you swim like fish. Now go to Weinshauks." He gave John a friendly push.

John trotted most of the two miles to his village. He was warm and dry by the time he reached Wegun's lodge.

"Cheegut!" she exclaimed. "You did remember what I told you." She put her arm around his bare shoulders. "And you are warm."

"I'm glad I didn't have to stay where the boys left me," John said. "The mosquitoes were thick and very hungry."

"What a good joke to play on them!" Wegun said, and she laughed.

"Have the boys come back?" John asked.

"They have not. Where did they take you?"

"We went to the north, then east through swamps and woods, then south to the shores of the sound," John said.

"Then you swam across the harbor and ran back here to Weinshauks," Wegun said. "You'll make a good red man. The boys will not be back for a long while. They will go back around the harbor and wade the upper end."

Some time later John heard them return. As they came toward the lodge he peeped out to see them. They were sweaty and very dirty. Mud crusted their moccasins and leggings. Blackberry and cat-brier thorns had scratched their bodies. Wegun stepped out to speak to them.

"Did you catch any of the long-billed shore birds?" she asked.

The boys whooped with laughter. Duksors said, "We caught a big one. He sits with an empty basket and a smoky torch while the mosquitoes sing to him and keep him company."

"Is this the basket?" Wegun asked as she reached into the doorway and handed it to the boys.

"It is!" shouted Bopoose. "How did you get it?"

"Your shore bird turned out to be a water bird," Wegun said as she patted his head.

John came to the doorway to enjoy the joke with Wegun.

The boys stared at him. "How did you get here so

quickly?" Duksors asked. "We left you there on the beach. We could still see the torch when we crossed the stream at the head of the harbor."

"I left it there to keep the mosquitoes warm," John said without a smile. "Then I came home by the shortest way, across the harbor."

"Yes," Wegun said. "Cheegut, the sea trout, swam over while the shore birds waded through the mud and briers."

During the next few days John found out who had planned the snipe hunt. He heard the other boys ask him if he wanted to hunt shore birds again. Duksors laughed as hard as any of them and grinned at John.

When they found out that Kiswis had followed them that night, they laughed and rolled in the sand. "He was going to creep up behind you to hurt you," said Bopoose. "Then he found only the torch burning there alone. Many mosquitoes died that night from drinking Kiswis's blood."

Each day, for the next few weeks, John could feel new strength. He found that he could swim farther, run without tiring, and hold his own in the simple hand wrestling of the Indian boys. He did not try the form that Hoskins had taught him. *Someday I'll teach them the 'catch-as-catch-can' that he taught me. They are the holds that help to win. Now if I learn the things that seem to come easy to the boys, I can have a chance to get away and find the trail back to Wethersfield.*

One morning, when they were playing together, John said, "Let's go to the woods more than we do. I'd like to know how to be a good redskin."

"You'll never be as good as a redskin," said Cujep. "We were born knowing."

For the next few days they made a game of finding things hidden in the woods. While some were hunting, others would crawl up and surprise them. John would try to work his way through the thick underbrush and leaves, only to find that several boys had surrounded him without his knowing it. "There you are, Cheegut," they would shout.

"You make more noise than a bear," said Bopoose. "Don't push so hard and fast. Try not to move anything as you slide through."

One day, as the boys were playing on the shore of the stream, hand wrestling and pushing each other about, Kiswis appeared. He glared at them and they stopped their play to draw aside and watch. Kiswis strutted over to where John was standing at the water's edge.

"You are named Cheegut!" he shouted, glaring at John. "Let me see you swim." He seized John to throw him into the stream.

John slipped from the young sanop's grasp and watched his opponent closely.

He met the next attack with a hip lock that spun the brave over the bank and into the stream, with a great splash.

The boys shouted. As Kiswis crawled out with water streaming from him, they laughed until he glared at them, then they were suddenly silent. His face was twisted with rage as he approached John once more. His eyes were narrowed to slits.

Kiswis was as tense as a coiled spring. Then he leaped, with clawed fingers, reaching for John's throat. The white boy swung to one side, grabbed the Indian's arm, and, using it is a lever, heaved him head over heels back into the stream.

"Yah! Yah!" screamed the boys as they ran along the bank to watch Kiswis splash his way out of the water. "You should be named 'Frog,' " one of them shouted. "You jump in and out like one."

Kiswis crawled out on the bank, rubbing his arm and sputtering. This time he did not charge at John, but circled to get back of him. The white boy turned to face him while the others stood back in a wide semicircle to watch. Everything was quiet except for the angry breathing of the young sanop.

Then, like a flash, Kiswis reached for a stone and threw it. John ducked as it whizzed past his ear. Then he closed in with clenched fists. Kiswis rushed at him and clutched for his throat, but John dodged. He swung, with all his weight behind his fist, at the point of his opponent's jaw. He could feel the jar of the blow all the way to his chest muscles. Kiswis stood for a second, staring into space, then he slowly crumpled and fell to the ground.

The boys circled around the unconscious sanop. Then they turned to John, examined his fist as if it were some strange weapon, and muttered to each other. He looked at Kiswis with as much wonder as the boys had shown. "Master Hoskins told me that was a knockout blow, but I never had to use it before."

"Kiswis will never forget." Cujep shook his head.

"We'll always remember," Cocheat said, and the boys crowded about John to put their hands on his shoulders. "We'll help you when you need it. He is a bad enemy to have."

John was the first to think of reviving the unconscious brave. He brought water from the stream and bathed the sanop's face. When Kiswis opened his eyes, he glared at the white boy and struggled to his feet. He shook off John's offer to help. Then he rubbed the back of his neck and staggered toward the village.

"You be careful, Cheegut," Cocheat said. "Kiswis is as mean and crafty as a snake. We are your friends and we will help you to watch him. We do not fear him. Not now."

The boys jumped and shouted as they trooped back to the village. For a while John was quiet, then he said, "I couldn't help myself, I should like to be his friend, but he would not let me after our fight was over and I tried to help him."

Chapter Four

PLANS TO ESCAPE

JOHN came through the gateway at Weinshauks, hardly noticing where he was going. He was brought up suddenly by a voice saying, "Hi, Cheegut. You go for long walk?" The sentry grinned at him. "By and by you may be like red man. Go to woods to hunt and fish. Remember, muckachuck, no red man walks in his dreams if he wants to keep his scalp."

John nodded and moved into the fort. *I was dreaming,* he thought. *Dreaming of how to get to Wethersfield. Now that I can come and go without being stopped, maybe I can get away.*

He stood inside the gate and thought of his life back at the settlement. His duty was plain, he must obey the orders of Governor Winthrop. Master Hoskins may have been a hard man, driving himself as he did others, but he had taught him many things in those brief periods between tasks. As for Mistress Hoskins, she had no time to spare as did the sachem's wife. In spite of her hard work, she had been kind to him and had nursed him when he was sick.

It was good fun to be with the Indian boys, but he wanted something beyond that. Life wasn't all play.

I wish I knew what it is all about. Why was I captured?

What are they going to do with me?

Then he remembered that Mommenoteck had told him to come back if he was troubled.

I wonder if he can tell me the reason.

The old sachem was sitting in the sun as if he had not moved since John had spoken to him. He opened his eyes and said, "I have been waiting for you. I knew you would come. Sit beside me on the mat and tell me what troubles you."

"Why did Kithansh and his raiding party take me prisoner?" John asked as he took his seat beside the old sachem.

"It is a long story, Cheegut. Two springs ago, at the time of the new oak leaves and the windflowers, Kiehtan was angry with his children. He turned his face away. Hobbamuck, the evil one, struck down our people. He made them to lie down with great sores and dry mouths. They died on their sleeping mats.

"Then the bearded white men and their squaws came to help. They dug graves for those who died and lined them with mats. It was as we should have done.

"Their Great Spirit must have loved them because no brave or squaw among them sickened, even when they nursed our sick and washed their bodies."

"I heard about the great plague of smallpox," John said.

"Wegun had two sons. The elder would have been about your age had he lived. He looked very much like you. When he joined the Great Spirit, Wegun was sad. He would never be tested as a man and a warrior. For a time she ate nothing. We thought that she did not sleep, for her eyes lost their brightness.

"After many days she took food and worked at her

woman's tasks for the sake of the remaining son, Nemud. We never saw her smile. All about her grieved.

"Then Kithansh felt sorrow for both the little brother and for the empty-hearted mother. He thought that a son, to fill the place of the one who died, would console her. It is the custom among the red men to do this, either with children from the tribe who have been made orphans, or by capture. There were no boys of noble blood who could be adopted.

"Many moons later, when he was hunting far up the great river, he saw you, who look so much like the lost one. He watched for many days, while his companions hunted across the river. He was sure you were the right one."

"I didn't see any red men near the farm," John said.

"He was there for many days. No white person can see Kithansh if he wishes to be hidden.

"When you stopped to comfort the papoose, Wegun smiled for the first time since her loss. Now it is as of old. Every kind act of yours brings gladness to those of us who like Wegun. Kithansh walks proudly because he has found the cure for her sorrow.

"Now Nemud looks up to you as to an elder brother. He walks like you. He wants to be with you at all times. You must never lead him along the wrong trail."

"I wondered about the little fellow. He was always at my heels," John said. "I didn't want to chase him away but sometimes I was afraid he would get hurt. I can see now, he was trying to be like the older boys."

"He was trying to be like you, Cheegut. It is sometimes the fortune for some of us to have one who watches and copies. Each of us, so chosen, must answer to the Great

Spirit if he fails.

"Soon you will have a ceremonial cleansing. We believe you will be a good member of the Pequotoog. Then, if Wegun desires, you will take the place of her lost son.

"When you can prove yourself a man, you will be given many chances to win honor. This you can surely do because your body is strong and your heart is good. You must learn the ways of the woods, the streams and the sea. When you become a sanop, a fighting name will be found for you."

"When we were talking last time," John said, "you told of those called 'strangers' who could never be sanops or sit in council."

"As Wegun's adopted son you would be a prince and be called a sachem." The old man nodded as if in weariness, and John stood up to go. "The trail to my lodge is always open, Cheegut," he said, and closed his eyes.

As John left, he thought of the future that had been mapped out for him. *If I were an Indian, this would be wonderful. But I'm white.*

He recalled that Master Hoskins had said, "The work is hard for all of us, but it will be worth it. Wethersfield and Hartford will grow because we labor to do it. Six years from now, when you become a man, you'll be glad you had a part in it."

John had a hard time getting to sleep that night. He thought of plan after plan; how to find a trail back to Wethersfield; what preparations to make. He knew he must either go along with the Pequot plans or make his escape. Getting back seemed to be his only course. He finally fell asleep.

When he awoke he could hear the usual morning stir. The serving squaw was blowing the fire into life, and smoke billowed out into the lodge.

Wegun came to his bed and said, "What is it that troubles you? Last night you muttered in your sleep. You cried out as if you were attacked by wild beasts."

John looked away for a moment. Then he said, "It is nothing. I feel better now."

During his breakfast he thought of the things he would need: a blanket, food for the journey, knowledge of the trails. The last would be the hardest.

He started by saving a bit of food from the meal. *I'll need enough for three days*, he thought, *maybe more if I have to hide on the way.* He slipped the dried food into his pouch.

During the morning he found a tree with a good-sized hole in it. The opening was covered with bushes and it was filled with dead wood and litter. He cleaned it out and lined it with dry grass. *I feel better with the pouch here instead of in the lodge. Each day I'll put in a handful of dried corn, smoked meat, or quahaugs. There will soon be enough.*

One day he found a scorched blanket. *Some squaw must have put this away to mend,* he thought. *Now all I need is to find my way.*

One day he talked with Wunx. John had often questioned him on woodcraft and following a trail. "What tribes are out there?" John said as he pointed to the north and to the west.

Wunx looked at him for a moment and then said, "Toward the setting sun are the Mohegans, known as the

'Man-eaters.' Beyond are the Quinnebaugs and the Waba-quassets." He swung his arm toward the north. "There are the Nipmucks. Why do you ask? Do you want to go there and fight them?" Wunx smiled.

"No, I don't want to fight," John answered. "The fish wants to know about streams and rivers that lead to the sea."

"Does the fish want to know who would catch him if he swims too far?"

"No. It's good to know where the sanops go to catch fish."

"That is a quick answer," said Wunx. "There are plenty of streams and good fish. The Pequotoog catch most of their fish in nets near the sound, but when we go north—no one dares stop us."

"Can I go fishing with you sometime?" John asked.

Wunx nodded.

Kiswis seemed to have forgotten his hostility to John. One day the white boy asked him, "Do the Pequotoog go hunting soon?"

"We hunt when the game is fat. That is before the deep snows," he answered.

"Do you go as far as the land of the Nipmucks when you hunt?"

"We don't go into the woods of the Nipmucks or the Mohegans. We have our hunting grounds and they have theirs."

"Do you stay away because the Pequotoog fear them?"

"We fear no one!" snarled Kiswis as he turned to leave John. "If we wish to go to their woods we go. The Man-eaters run. They fear us. They would feed you to their dogs because your flesh is not sweet like that of a red man."

Some of the older sanops seemed pleased when John asked questions.

"There is a broad trail to the land of the Nipmuck," said Nausipouck. "Across the Pequot River is the land of the Mohegan. Six hours' journey from here the trail divides. The broad trail to the right leads to the Nipmucks. It is easy to follow. The left-hand trail is faint because we have little to do with the Mohegans and the Podunks."

"Is Machemoodus in the land of the Mohegans?" John asked.

Nausipouck shivered. "We do not speak of the evil place. It lies in the land of the Podunks and there are many small lakes near it. There is no trail. No one travels that way."

The next evening, as they squatted at their meal, Mononotto said to Wegun, "Tomorrow, Sassacus sends Kithansh and his party to Ninigret."

"Is there trouble with the Niantics?" said Wegun.

"It is not bad. Some of the Niantics have been getting fish and quahaugs in the Pequot coves and streams. Kithansh is to warn them."

"I have heard nothing of this," said Wegun. "All Weinshauks hears when plans like this are made. The squaws talk."

"It has been known to only a few," Mononotto said. "We have young sanops who would cry out for a raid if they knew. The party leaves quietly at daybreak. Nothing must be told." He looked at John and Nemud. Then he repeated, "Nothing must be told."

John had trouble finishing his meal. *I may never have*

a chance like this again, he thought. *Kithansh and the sanops with him are the best trackers in Weinshauks. They cannot get back before the next day.* He gulped the rest of his food and went out into the night.

He walked about the fort for a while as he tried to calm himself. The stars were clear but not too bright. "When they stand out so you can almost touch them, it means bad weather," Nausipouck had said.

Tomorrow I'll have the morning meal and then slip away, John thought. *It will be good to be a white boy once more, even if it means hard work. Here the sanops speak of fighting, taking scalps, and killing white people. Even the boys talk that way. The men do not try to build and make living better. They think only of war.*

But many are good. My leaving will hurt Wegun and Nemud. Maybe the Hoskins miss me.

Everything is confused—but in one way my duty seems clear. I must return to Wethersfield.

John went back to the lodge and was soon asleep.

Chapter Five

THE FLIGHT

JOHN awoke the next morning and peered out of the doorway. There was a glow in the eastern sky. Mist was rising from the stream. *It will be a good day to travel,* he thought as he put on his clothes.

He forced himself to eat, and he didn't dare speak. Wegun looked at him several times but did not break in on his thoughts.

"Come with us to the swimming place," called Duksors as the other boys waited a short distance away. "We want to try some more of your tricks in the water."

"I don't feel like swimming now," John said. The boys stared at him.

"Cheegut must be sick, if he does not wish to swim," Duksors said. The boys looked at each other, shrugged, and walked away toward the gate. They moved slowly and looked back to see if John would change his mind.

After they had gone, John picked up his shirt and leggings and strolled through the gate. He walked a short distance and then knelt, pretending to tie a thong on his moccasin. As he crouched there, he looked about him but could see no one in sight. When he was sure he was not being watched, he slipped into the nearby bushes and crawled to his hollow tree.

He felt in the hole and gasped. There was no blanket. His pouch was untied and empty. The hunting bow had its string cut and the arrows were broken.

John swallowed hard. "This is another of Kiswis's dirty tricks. But I cannot stop now. I must go on without these things."

He set off through the woods to find the great trail. He skirted the swamp called "Homowauke" and headed toward the thick woods. He covered his trail as well as he could in his haste. *I'll be safe if I can get a good head start,* he thought. *They can follow my trail so I won't spend too much time covering it.*

He pushed his way through the undergrowth. Branches slashed at him and thorns clawed his leggings. He reached the great trail sooner than he expected.

It was a clear track, well beaten by moccasined feet. It followed the ridges and the high ground along the east side of the river. He now ran with ease, his empty pouch flapping against his side. Each hour carried him nearer the land of the Nipmucks.

Back there, when he was in too much of a hurry to stop, there were plenty of bushes loaded with huckleberries. Now it would be a job to find anything to help fill his stomach. John was thankful for his Indian training that had taught him to eat when he could and, when there was no food, to tighten his belt and keep going.

He halted at a grove of white birch to gather tender young shoots to put in his pouch. A little farther along he found a sassafras tree and gathered twigs, buds, and leaves. Elderberry from a swamp and wintergreen leaves with berries just forming went into the pouch until it bulged.

It was nearly nightfall when he reached the stream that Nausipouck said was the boundary of the Nipmucks' land. He had a moment of despair. *I've passed the trail to Machemoodus. The sachem said it was faint and I've missed it. Now I can't hide out where they are afraid to follow.*

He parted the bushes and brushed out any traces he had made. Then he moved down the stream and found a place where he could curl up in a pile of dead leaves. He ate some berries and tender twigs, drank from the stream, and was soon asleep.

A ray from the rising sun slanted through the leaves and fell on John's face. He was awake in a moment and looked about him from his hiding place. Birds were chirping in the nearby trees. A towhee scratched in the dry leaves. John saw a squirrel run up a nearby tree without stopping to scold. *If there were Indians near there would be more excitement than this,* he thought.

He searched the woods near the brook and found some berries, which he ate for his morning meal. He picked a few more for his pouch, then set to work to conceal his sleeping place.

"When the stream turns north, we leave it and keep on toward the setting sun," Wunx had told him. "Soon we find another stream, starting from a large pond. This empties into the great river." The sanop had looked at him in a strange manner as he marked the course with a stick.

Wunx will look for me here, John thought. *I wonder if*

I should change my course. Then he set out along the stream. *I have a day's head start. Besides, I might get lost if I left this stream.*

The traveling was getting harder. The bushes that lined the stream were thick and often thorny. The stream bed was worse because the rocks were smooth and slippery. He had several falls before he decided to look for better footing on the ground away from the water. Here he found a deer track and was able to follow it at a slow trot.

When he reached the northward turning of the stream, he struck off to the west, keeping his shadow in front of him. As the sun rose higher he searched for the pond that Wunx had described. It fed the stream that he wanted to follow.

He was hungry. He could almost smell cakes of corn meal wrapped in leaves and baked in the hot ashes, or a stew of meat and groundnuts thickened with flour of dried acorns. A few berries and tender twigs were not enough. Then he remembered what Kithansh had said, "A red man eats when he can. He fills himself with food and stores up its strength. When he has no food he uses that strength even while hungry. Hunger is not starving."

The bushes about him seemed to be getting greener. They were so thick that John had to push his way through them. Then suddenly he broke through to see a long pond in front of him. Off to the right it stretched with many coves and a few small islands. To his left he could hear the sound of running water. He waded along the shore toward this sound and in a few hundred paces came to an outlet where the water of the lake tumbled over rocks to form a stream. That stream boiled its way toward the west.

John knelt and dipped water to his mouth with a cupped hand. He smiled when he remembered what Kithansh had told him. "White man puts his face in the water to drink in fish and frogs. Red man comes behind and there is another scalp to hang on his belt." He felt that a few fish and frogs might be welcome—in fact, anything to eat.

The stream became wider and ran more smoothly. John found another deer run, and the traveling became easier. His spirits rose as he hurried along. As the sun was getting low he suddenly came out into the open and saw the broad water of the Connecticut River ahead of him.

He crouched on the shore, hidden in a clump of bushes, and looked across to the opposite bank. He planned how he would swim the slow current and where he would land.

As the darkness started to close in, he thought of the hard work ahead of him on the Hoskins farm. As he remembered it the work was harder than that of the Pequots' slaves. Wegun was kind and he had never had so much fun as with the Indian boys. *Shall I ever see Duksors or Bopoose again? I'll miss Cujep and Cocheat and especially little Nemud.*

He was untying his moccasin when he heard a sound that made him stop and remain motionless. A blue jay screamed and a red squirrel set up an angry chatter.

John remained silent. He wondered if the wild things had discovered him. He squatted there praying that he was the one who created the alarm. Then from a short distance he heard a voice calling, "Aque, Cheegut." It was the voice of Kithansh.

John felt weak all over. Across the river he could see a roof with smoke curling from the chimney. There were white people just an easy swim away.

If it were only dark I might get to the water and out-swim them. Then he caught a glimpse of a bark canoe pulled up on the shore and partly concealed with branches.

I can never make it swimming. And I'll never have another chance. Maybe he hasn't seen me and is calling to make me answer—that's an Indian trick. He remained silent.

"*Wesassu!*" called the mocking voice of Kiswis.

Yes, I am afraid. John could hear the snapping of dry twigs on all sides, as if his pursuers wanted him to know that he was surrounded. *If I get to the river they will catch me in their canoe. I'll not move.*

"Why did you try to run away from us?" called Kithansh. "We see you hidden in the bushes. Stand up and come to me."

John stepped out of his hiding place. He could see that escape was hopeless. All about him the foliage moved and one after another the sanops appeared. Kithansh rose a few paces from him. On the other side was Wunx. Tulepas and Wahsus were between him and the woods. Kiswis leered at him from a short distance up the stream bed. It was hard to endure the triumph of Kiswis, but worse than this was Kithansh's look of disappointment.

"You traveled fast," said Kithansh, "but it was wrong for you to try to leave us. We trusted you."

John knew that he could not explain why he had to return to the white people. "I was bound by the law of the English," he said. "I must obey."

"Soon there will be no more English," Kithansh said. "We shall drive all white people away or destroy them

67

along with their laws. This is the land of the red man and we shall have it back for our own."

He came over and put his hand on John's shoulder. "You were one of us, almost Wegun's son. Someday you would have been a sanop—the son of Mononotto. Now all is changed."

"He never would have been a good red man," Kiswis said with a sneer. "See how easy it was for us to track him down."

"Five sanops to track one boy! Few red men could outwit us, the best of the Pequot trackers!" Kithansh said. "He would have been a good Pequot if all of us had been his friends. You, Kiswis, have been his enemy from the start. When he defended himself against you, you hated him. You have done much to make him want to leave us."

"Wonnux!" shouted Kiswis. "It was I who stole your food from the hollow tree. I took the blanket back to the squaw. I cut your bowstring and broke your arrows. I hope you are hungry and eaten by mosquitoes."

Kithansh looked up with a start. "Are you hungry? Here, take and eat." He opened his pouch and handed it to John.

It was the boy's first satisfying food in two days. He chewed on the parched corn and dried quahaugs.

"You moved fast," said Wunx. "When we came back from Ninigret last night and found you gone, we ate and then took the light canoe. We have paddled all night and this morning. Then we rested. Now you rest, while we paddle to our camping place."

"Tomorrow we go back to Weinshauks," said Kithansh.

As they climbed into the light craft, Wahsus took his

place in the stern. "Now we watch Cheegut all the time," he said. "He won't have a chance to run away again."

They started shortly after dawn and paddled steadily all day, stopping only for a sip of water or a handful of parched corn.

The sun was low over the hills when they reached Weinshauks. Smoke rose from the cooking fires, and sanops squatted near the doorways waiting. They looked at John and then turned away.

He met one of the boys and said, "Aque Cujep." The young Indian stared at him and then off beyond. Duksors and Bopoose dodged back of one of the lodges as he came near. Only Cocheat spoke. He grunted and spat on the ground at John's feet.

As he approached Wegun's lodge she came to the door and stood there. "So you came back?" she said. "But not because you wanted to. What are we to think of a son who breaks our hearts?"

John hung his head. "I'm sorry I hurt you," he said. "You and Mononotto have been good to me."

"Then why did you leave us that way?"

"The court in Massachusetts ordered that I stay with the Hoskins until I became a man. It is the law of the English and I am English."

"But they made you work like a slave. You had no time to play."

"It is true that I worked hard, but much of it was something I wanted to do. I like to plant things and see them grow. Each year the house was better because of the work we did on it. Master Hoskins taught me to use tools made of steel, but he watched closely because saw and chisel are precious. We were getting ready to build a shed for the cow."

"Much of this is squaw's work," Wegun said. "Here in Weinshauks, the things that seemed like play helped to train you for the life of a sanop. Did you learn to hunt game and defend your home? Did you learn how to loose an arrow or throw a tomahawk?"

"I was taught to defend myself—I showed that with Kiswis. Master Hoskins also showed me how to swim. I have been able to hold my own with the boys of the village. I can't be a sanop and go on the warpath against my own people."

"There would be no need to fight the wonnux. We have other enemies. You could win much honor." Wegun stood aside and motioned to John.

"Come. Your bed is as you left it and you are welcome to stay with us," she said. "Your friends, here in Weinshauks, will forgive you, but they cannot forget. Many, who are not your friends, will look on you as another wonnux. You must be on your guard."

John returned to the life of a Pequot, but soon found how true Wegun's words were. The boys accepted his running away as another adventure. He was happy with this until the day they started on a hunting trip with bows and arrows. Cocheat said, "You go back to the village, white boy. We go too far into the woods."

Each day it became plainer that he was a prisoner. Several times he wandered alone toward the woods, and each time a sanop would appear and motion him back toward the fort.

He was glad they let him keep his bow. He restrung it

with twisted sinew, got new arrows, and practiced shooting at a mark.

One of the older sanops, Wincumbone, found him with his bow and watched for a while. "You jerk the string with your fingers, white boy," he said. "Let it slip from them. Here, let me have the bow. I'll show you."

He took the bow, fitted an arrow to the string, and drew till the feathers touched his jawbone. "Now let it roll from your fingers like this." The bowstring twanged and the arrow quivered in the target.

"That is good bow," the sanop said as he handed it back to John. "An Indian would do good work with it. White people never shoot well with bow and arrow." Then he stalked away.

He never heard of Robin Hood or the English bowmen at Crécy, John thought. *I'll show him an English boy can shoot.*

Each day he practiced until he was sure that his arrow would come close to the mark. Mononotto nodded his approval when he brought wild pigeons and rabbits for their meals. John was grateful to the sanop for his advice. He searched for Wincumbone to tell him.

When John found the old sanop, he was seated at the door of his lodge with several large chunks of wood about him. A small fire glowed near him and he was busy with a stone chisel, scraping charred wood from the center of a block he held on his knees.

"It was good of you to show me how to use the bow," John said. "Now I can shoot small animals and pigeons for our food."

"You can hit pigeons?" the sanop said. "That is good

71

for a white boy."

John squatted on the ground to watch. "You are making a bowl?" he asked.

The sanop worked without answering. After a time he said, "First you pick wood that will not crack. The tall swamp trees with dark wood sometimes have bumps on them. These make good bowls. Now watch."

He placed a glowing coal in the hollow and blew on it until the wood smoked. Then he dumped the coal back in the fire and scraped the charred placed until it showed unburned wood.

"It takes much time to make a bowl," he said. "Few of us can do it well." He reached into the doorway, picked up a finished bowl, and handed it to John. It was as big as Mistress Hoskins' mixing bowl and it shone with a dull glow.

"I made that. White men call the wood 'black gum.' "

"It is good," John said as he rubbed his hand over the smooth surface. "Where can I get some of this wood?"

"These came from Homowauke," the sanop said. "They are hard to find. You chop lumps like this from the trees with your tomahawk."

"The Pequots will not let me go as far as the swamp," John said. He stood up to go.

"Here, white boy, take this small one." The sanop reached for a chunk that seemed to be hopelessly misshapen. "Take this to play with. If you spoil it there is little loss." He searched among his stone chisels and handed one to John. "This is not a good one. You can make a new edge when you rub it on a rock. Keep it."

John could not think of any Indian word for "thanks."

He said, "It is good." The sanop nodded and went on scraping.

For several days John worked on the bowl He picked a place away from the lodge and carried coals from the hearth to kindle his fire.

He put a coal in the hollow he had made and blew on it until the smoke from the charred wood stung his eyes. Then he scraped with his stone chisel until the inside was smooth and brown. It was no longer a crooked knot. He was turning the bowl around in his hands, feeling its surface, when a shadow fell across his work. He looked up to see Mononotto standing there. "How did Cheegut learn to make bowls?" he said as he reached for John's work. He turned it around to see that it was true. "It is good work."

"Wincumbone showed me. He gave me the wood and this scraper."

"He is our best bowl maker," the sachem said. He handed the unfinished bowl back to the boy. "What will you do with it when it is finished?"

"If it is good I'll give it to Wegun. That is, if she will have it."

"We'll say nothing of this until you are ready," Mononotto said.

After the evening meal John heard Wegun and Mononotto talking.

"Cheegut is trying hard to be a good red man," said Mononotto. "He has brought game for our food. He shoots well with the bow."

"He is unhappy," Wegun replied. "He came to us too late. You cannot tame a wild animal if he is too old—he will always go back to his own kind. Let us send him back to the white people at Wethersfield."

"He has been with the Pequotoog too long to let him go now. He knows too much about us."

"Cheegut will never turn against us," Wegun said.

"I know what a white boy would have to do. When we go on the warpath against the wonnux he will have to take sides. He knows our trails, the way our fort is defended, and our language. He would use all of this, if need be, to save his own people. No, Cheegut must stay."

"Have any of our sanops done anything to make him feel that he belongs here? Everyone distrusts him. Even the boys are different. He cannot go far with them so he wanders alone much of the time."

"He brought it on himself," said Mononotto, "but he has found some who are ready to help him." Then his voice was so low that John could hear no more until Wegun said, "That will be good."

A few days later the bowl was shaped and John smoothed it with a bit of leather and fine sand. Then he oiled it and rubbed it to a hard, smooth finish with a piece of bone. He had seen Hoskins rub his musket butt in this way.

When he handed it to Wegun, she said, "Where did you get this pretty bowl? Who gave it to you?"

"I made it. Wincumbone showed me how and gave me the wood."

"That was good of him. You are a good workman." She called to Mononotto, "Look what Cheegut has given me."

Mononotto pushed the curtain aside and came toward them. He nodded to John and took the bowl from Wegun. "It's better than I thought," he said.

"Then you knew that he was making it," said Wegun.

"Yes. It was to be a surprise."

"That is why you—" She paused.

"Yes, that is only one of many reasons," the sachem replied. "His heart is good and so is his work. He should have good tools, and more friendship."

Chapter Six

THE TALKING LEAVES

JOHN could see the squaws off in the distance, gathering huckleberries. Near the fort were mats covered with berries drying in the sun for the winter's use. The women gathered them in at night, before the evening dampness could undo their work, and then spread them again each morning until the berries were shriveled and hard. Several baskets of these were already stored.

The boys had gone to the shore of the sound to fish with pointed sticks. John knew better than to try to go with them.

He sat near the entrance to the lodge and stared off into space. *No place to go, nothing to do,* he thought, *not even a chance to get away.* He picked up some pebbles and rolled them toward a cricket to see him jump.

Mononotto came to the door and looked at him. Then he went back. In a moment he returned and handed John a package wrapped in birch bark and tied with sinew. "This is for you, Cheegut. It is well that you have it." Then he walked away, across the dancing place.

John untied the knot, to save the cord, and unwrapped the bark. Lying inside was a knife over two spans long, and with it was a sheath decorated with quill embroidery. He fitted the wooden handle into his fist and tested the edge of the knife with his thumb. "It's good English steel," he said. "And it is mine." He fastened the sheath to his belt where he could reach for the handle. There was a thong to fasten around his leg so he could draw the knife quickly.

John looked for Mononotto to thank him, but he was nowhere to be found. He went into the lodge to show Wegun.

"Mononotto got the knife from a red man who had it in trade from the English. There was no blood price paid for it. The design on the sheath is Narragansett. You may need friends among my people and this will help you get them," Wegun said. "Now the boys will envy you."

John tried out his knife on soft wood. He carved spoons and stirring paddles, modeling them after the utensils in Prudence Hoskins' kitchen.

Wegun was pleased with them. "This is the work of a man," she said. "Baskets and weaving by women, but men carve bowls and spoons."

A few days later he was sitting in the doorway of the lodge, busy with his new craft, when a runner arrived. Mononotto came out to greet him. "You have come from the Narragansett fort," he said. "What brings you here in such haste?"

"I bring news. It is bad," said the messenger. "It is for you or Sassacus to hear."

"Come with me," Mononotto said. They moved out of John's hearing, and the sachem listened intently.

Then the sachem said, "Sassacus must hear this at once. He will call a council to hear what you have to tell. You have done well." They walked toward the king's lodge.

Soon a messenger ran from lodge to lodge, calling the more important members of the council to meet with Sassacus.

"Let us go to the great lodge and lie in the grass outside, near the wall," said Nemud. "I've done it often. If it's secret they will drive us away and no harm will be done. If it's not secret, they may let us stay, if we keep quiet. There may be much excitement."

Each of them selected a spot where he could lie on his stomach and see through a crack between the bark slabs. Several of the sachems looked their way but went into the council room without speaking to them.

He could see Sassacus reclining on a pile of mats. He had on his beaded cap and feather mantle and held his ceremonial war club in his hand. When the council had assembled, John saw the king motion with the club toward the messenger.

The Indian rose and raised his hand in salute. "You know that I have lived among the Narragansetts as a 'stranger.' I did work that is not well for a sanop to do, but I did it to serve the Pequotoog, my people. In the past I have brought you much news that you found to be true. Now I bring word of that which means great trouble for the 'Destroyers.' Hear, and do not blame me for being the carrier of evil words.

"Miantonomo, who rules with the old king, Canonicus, went with other Narragansetts on a mission to the head sachem of the wonnux at Shawmut. This place is called 'Boston' by the whites. With him were the grandsons of Canonicus and twenty sanops. Cutshamakin, a sachem of the Massachusetts, had brought word that the wonnux wished to do them honor. Cutshamakin went with them because he is able to speak in both tongues.

"When they reached Shawmut in their long canoe, many wonnux, in shining coats and carrying bushkeagun, came to meet them. They led the red men to the great council house, beating on their war drums and walking in step. There they exchanged gifts and sat down to a feast of strange food.

"After the feast there was much talk. A treaty came of it which bound the wonnux, and the Narragansetts with all their allies, to help the English destroy the Pequotoog. They, in turn, promised to help the red men who were loyal to them."

The spy paused for a moment and Sassacus said, "What was this treaty? Can you tell us what was said?"

"I can, O King. There were nine things which I have remembered by my fingers and one thumb."

He continued, holding up finger after finger as he told each item:

"A firm peace between the English and all red men who wish to be friends and allies.

"No one to make peace with the Pequotoog unless all agree.

"No one to give shelter or help any Pequot.

"To put to death, or turn over to the English, any Pequot who has killed a white person.

"Not to hide any white servants who run away from their masters. These are to be returned to the English to be punished."

Nemud nudged John and said, "They mean you, Cheegut."

"That the English shall give the Narragansetts word when they are about to attack the Pequotoog. The Narragansetts promise, in turn, to give guides who will lead the English along the trails into our country.

"No red man is to come near a wonnux house or farm during the war, which is to come, without carrying the 'talking leaves' from the white men saying that he may do so.

"Two moons after the war with the Pequotoog is ended, to send a present to the English."

Then, holding up his thumb, "And the last: that this peace is to be from father to son and to son's son so long as the earth shall be.

"When the Narragansetts went to their canoe to depart, the English braves came with them and made their bushkeagun speak in farewell. I heard one sanop say that no one could stand against these warriors, who killed from far off and cannot be hurt by our arrows."

There had been angry murmurs during this recital, but Indian courtesy permitted the speaker to finish without interruption. Now there was a rush of indignant words.

Sassacus sat erect and said, "Let there be silence! We cannot fight the wonnux and the enemy red men here in the council room with our tongues. Let us plan a way to win back our own kind so that we may make a stand against these whites."

He turned to the spy. "How do you know what was said by the English at Shawmut? It was far away. You could not hear it."

The spy drew himself to his full height and said, "Because I heard the 'talking leaves.' Miantonomo asked, as our king has asked, 'How do we know that you English will remember this and hold to it? We must be sure you will stand by us to the end. The white sachem repeated each thing to an English *powow* who made marks on the white leaves.

"The white sachem said to him, 'What is on the talking leaves is what we shall do. Have the White Father, whom we call Williams, read these to you. Remember what we have said and hear them again when they speak through him. You will know that we speak true. So long as the white leaves are with you they will give the same message.'

"It was so. The White Father came in his canoe when Canonicus sent for him. He looked at the magic and spoke the words I have remembered, because I heard him speak them. The Narragansett sanops looked at each other in wonder. Miantonomo said, 'It is so.' "

"Then we must fight them all!" shouted an angry sanop. "Let us dance about Guldooke and go on the warpath. Nothing can stand in the way of the Pequotoog."

"That is not the way," Mononotto said. "We must show Canonicus that the way of the talking leaves is the way to ruin for all red men. We must fight the English, if we do not wish to be wiped out, but to be at war with our own kind will weaken all red men so the English will take our land and make us all slaves."

"Mononotto speaks wisely," said Sassacus. "When they weaken the Pequotoog, it will then be the turn of the Narragansett. Soon there will be no red men left in the land which Kiehtan has given us. The wonnux will possess everything."

He stood up and drew his feathered cloak about him,

"Go. Prepare yourselves in every way for war with the whites that must come, but hold your hand until they are ready to strike. Do not stir up the hornets' nest until we are ready. We shall talk to old Canonicus. He has seen many winters and is wiser than his young men. He will hear our side and not be blinded by the shining coats and the smooth words of the wonnux."

"Canonicus is proud," added Mononotto. "He will never forget that he was humbled by the whites at Plymouth, fifteen winters ago. How can he love them after having been shamed and frightened in that manner?"

Chapter Seven

A FIRE IS KINDLED

It was late in the month that the white man called August. The last of the tall bush huckleberries had been gathered and set to dry in the sun. Now there were large blackberries growing thick in the tangled brambles on the sunny slopes near the village. John watched them turn from green to red and then to glossy black.

"Come with me, Nemud," he said one morning. "We'll pick some of the ripe berries and look for rabbits." He slung his hunting bow and a quiver of arrows over his shoulder. He tied the sheath of his knife around his leg so he could draw quickly, and practiced as he waited for the boy. The knife seemed to leap into his hand and cling there.

John could hear Nemud scurry around inside, and then he heard him say to Wegun, "I know it's squaw's work, but we are going to eat them and get rabbits, too." When he came out he had his bow slung just like John's and he pretended to reach for a knife at his side.

They pushed their way into the tangled bushes that reached over their heads in places. Nemud crammed the fruit into his mouth as fast as he picked it. Very few fell into his pail as he pushed deeper and deeper into the thickest part of the patch.

John picked steadily. He was ready at an instant to swing his bow and shoot at any small furry creature that darted out. Then he heard Nemud call, "Cheegut!"

He's met his match with the thorns. Let him untangle himself. John picked on without looking up.

"Cheegut!" Nemud screamed. "Cheegut! Help me!"

John looked back and reached for his bow. There, rising close to the boy, was the largest bear John had ever seen. Nemud stood still, staring at the beast as if he were charmed.

"Keep still, little brother," John called as calmly as he could. "Do not move. I'll try to make the bear come this way. When he leaves you, crawl very softly until you are away from him, then run to the village for the hunters."

As John spoke, the bear swung around and went down on all fours. John could see the branches swaying as the great beast pushed toward him. He waved his arms until he saw Nemud crawl from the edge of the thorns, then he shouted, "Run, Nemud, run!"

The bear reared up a few paces from John and stood, swaying from side to side. The white boy slowly fitted an arrow to the bowstring, drew the feathered nock to his cheek, and loosed it. He could see the light shaft strike and quiver in the animal's throat. The bear clawed at it with a huge paw and growled.

John fitted another arrow to the string and started to back. There was bloody froth dripping from the bear's mouth as he seemed about to turn away. Then he swung toward John, who loosed the second arrow and saw it strike

84

near the shoulder. The animal stopped to bite at it and gave John the chance to turn and try for the nearby trees.

As he ran, he reached for his knife and drew it. He had taken only a few steps when he felt a blow and burning pain as the bear raked his back. He fell to the ground and turned over with one arm covering his throat. The bear was on him in an instant and John stabbed and stabbed wherever he could. He felt a hot gush of blood and his knife was yanked from his hand. Then the bear fell on him.

John could hardly breathe. The furry bulk was still and it pressed him into the ground with its dead weight. He tried to move it, but it was too much for him. He lay still for a moment, trying to breathe. He felt his strength slipping away, so he dug at the soft ground beneath him and soon found that he could crawl out.

As he tried to get up, the ground and trees seemed to be rocking and twisting about him. He knew that he must get to the village for help. He crawled blindly up a slope that he felt must be the direction to the gate.

He wanted to call, but was too proud to show his weakness. He fell, with his face in the grass, and lay still.

Then, very dimly, he was aware of footsteps and a blur of sound. "Cheegut!" he heard a voice that sounded like Kithansh's. "What has the bear done to my young brother?" Gentle hands lifted him and he felt himself slipping away into darkness, but he smiled. Kithansh had again called him "young brother."

John did not know how long he had been unconscious, but when he did recover, he was aware that he was struggling back to a world of pain and strange sounds. He opened his eyes and found he was in his own bed with blankets heaped on him. Fire blazed from the central hearth. He turned his head to see better.

A tall figure that seemed to have emerged from his bad dreams was dancing in slow steps and singing. His voice was pitched as high and shrill as that of a squaw. As he stepped about in the cleared area, anklets of bone clattered. He kept time with the swish of pebbles in the turtle shell rattle. When he saw John move, he reached into a pouch and took out a handful of leaves which he threw into the fire. Choking smoke billowed out toward John. Then the figure danced toward him, waving his arms over the boy and swishing the smoke from John to the open door.

The song, which had been getting louder and more shrill, now rose to a high-pitched shriek.

John now recognized the figure as Wamposhet, the powow. *I've never seen him with his tall mask and feathers. I wish he'd stop.*

Wamposhet leaned over, took a deep breath, and blew in John's face. Then he went, with high steps, toward the doorway and out into the open. *I wish I could get out in the fresh air away from the smoke and stink.*

He was about to close his eyes again, when Wegun came and knelt beside the bed. "Oh, my Cheegut," she whispered. "We thought we had lost you. When you were carried in here, all covered with blood, I washed you and dressed the great wound on your back. You called for me but did not know me. Then you were still. You hardly breathed. We sent for Wamposhet to drive out the bad spirits that would have taken you from us."

"His song nearly drove me out of my mind. I was glad when he stopped."

"You must give thanks. He made good medicine. It caused you to open your eyes and know me once more. He pushed the bad spirits from your body and waved them from the lodge. Then he breathed good spirits into you."

"What about the bear?" John said. "Did they get him?"

"Our young men brought in the great bear. They lashed it fast to a long pole and eight of them carried it in to be skinned and cut up for a feast."

"Who is that singing the strange song?" John asked.

"That is Wahsus. Listen to what he is saying."

John caught a few of the words the young sanop was singing.

"—forgive the white boy. He killed to save the son of our sachem—do not come back in our dreams—give us the strength of your body when we feast." Then the strange chant stopped.

"Wahsus has now made peace with the bear's ghost," Wegun said. "It was his duty as a member of the Bear Clan to placate the animal you killed. Now he has saved us all from being frightened in our dreams. He will be happy, and will eat as much of the bear meat as anyone."

John looked through the doorway and saw a crowd of sanops. They were clustered about the body of the bear, reaching in to tap it with war clubs and tomahawks.

"They are getting strength from the bear by touching his body with their weapons," Wegun said. "They do this in battle, when a brave foe has been killed. The one who slew him takes the scalp while others strike the body to get some of the dead warrior's courage."

Nemud sat outside the doorway, keeping very still. John did not know he was there until he heard the boys ask, "Is Cheegut dead?"

Duksors peeped into the lodge.

"The bear could not kill my brother," said Nemud. "He is too strong. Someday I shall kill a bear."

"Can we go in to see Cheegut?" said Bopoose.

Wegun patted him on the shoulder. "No, he must rest so he can be at the feast tomorrow."

The boys scattered when Mononotto and Kithansh entered.

"Look, Wegun," the young sanop said. "The knife that Mononotto gave to the young brother. There were many wounds and the last one was in the bear's heart, where we found this."

"Never was a gift so well repaid as this," said Mononotto. "Now we have two sons instead of being childless."

"Go your way and let Cheegut rest." Wegun pulled the blankets around John's neck. "Don't you see that his face is getting hot? He must rest and gather strength." She whispered to John, "Sleep now. Tomorrow you shall sit up, in spite of pain, to have great honor at the feast."

It was hard to sleep. Pain and joy both kept him wide awake. Finally he drifted off to awaken in the early morning when Wegun knelt beside the bed to feel his forehead.

"The bear was a fat one," Wegun told John as she changed the dressing on his back. "It will make a great feast for all in the village."

"Will there be enough for all?" John asked. "He seemed

big when he stood up in front of me, but not big enough to feed everyone."

"The hunters have returned with game: fat deer, rabbits, birds. There are fish and clams from the shore. Then we have corncakes baked in the ashes. Yes, there will be plenty.

"All the village is talking about you, what a good red man you are. Nemud brags that he went for help while you fought. Someday he may even dream that he helped kill the great beast. Now some of the squaws are scraping the underside of the hide, and then they will cure it for you. When all the cuts are mended it will make a fine robe for a warrior. You will be that warrior."

"When do they feast?" John asked.

"Just after sundown today. The squaws have cut up the meat and are now preparing a stew. You will sit with the sanops when the bowls are passed around. Be tall and straight, no matter how much pain you feel. It is the way of the warrior."

That evening John sat with the sanops in the great circle about the fire. His young friends looked across at him, their eyes flashing in the firelight. An old sanop, the village orator, stood and told with many dramatic gestures about John's fight. How he had rescued the son of their sachem, Mononotto, and now sat without showing any sign of the pain he felt. The sanops nodded their heads and dipped into their stew. Many of them shouted, "Ho!"

In the midst of the feast a runner dashed into the village and came to the center of the circle. "I come from Sassacus," he said. "I have traveled far."

"You will sit and feast on bear meat," Kithansh said as he motioned to a place in the circle. "No messenger from our king shall speak while hungry."

"Sassacus is far to the west, near our border," the messenger said as he dipped into the steaming bowl. "He is troubled. I have his message to Mononotto. I give it when the sachem is ready to hear me."

"Fill yourself," Mononotto said. "When you have finished come to me."

The brave crammed food into his mouth, wiping his lips with the back of his hand. When he had finished he patted his tight stomach and said, "It is good. Bear meat is for warriors. Now I am strong." He rose and went to Mononotto's lodge.

The squaws and children were now feeding on the remains of the feast. John realized that the home life of Wegun and Mononotto was more like that of a white family than of an Indian one. Squaws did not usually eat with their husbands.

A messenger came from the sachem. He approached the members of the council, who rose and left the circle. Those who remained looked at each other with serious faces. There was no dancing or telling of stories. Finally they got up and went to their lodges.

The squaws stayed behind to clear up the remains of the feast. They scraped the bowls, saving bits of food for future use. That which seemed worthless they threw to the dogs, who fought and snarled over the bones and bits of sinew.

"Do not throw any bones in the fire," one old squaw said. "We do not wish to have Cheegut's bones ache, nor the bones of the other hunters."

When the conference was over, the Pequots gathered outside the great lodge to hear their leaders. Some were talking loudly, but most stood scowling.

John was back in his bed when Wegun came to him and said, "The news is bad. Young hotheads near Manisses, which the whites call Block Island, paddled out to the great winged canoe of the captain named Oldham. They said they wanted to trade, but when they got aboard they slew the captain and rolled his body in a fish net. The other white people shut themselves in the lodge aboard their craft. Then the foolish young men tried to set the wings to go back to their village at Manisses."

Mononotto entered the lodge and looked toward his wife. "Have you told Cheegut what troubles us?" he asked.

"Yes," Wegun replied. "It is good that he should know."

"There will be weeping in many lodges for what has happened," Mononotto said. "Many were slain."

"As the young men tried to sail the canoe, it fluttered about so strangely that a wonnux captain named Gallop sailed his canoe to see what was wrong. When he saw the red men, some of them sons of sachems, his men slew them with their bushkeagun and long knives. Then they threw the bodies overboard. One, only, escaped to swim ashore and hide at Manisses. Now the wonnux will gather like angry hornets and attack those at the island."

"Will the white men ask the Pequotoog to pay for those who have been slain on the canoe?"

"They will do that and more," Mononotto replied. "They will demand that we send the young brave who escaped, to be killed by them. That we cannot do. They have already had enough blood to pay for the lives of the man and boy who were slain."

"War and death will come," said Wegun. "We must stand by our own, even if they are wrong."

"If the wonnux would say, 'Punish your young men in your own way,' then we could keep our reckless ones from doing wrong. Now we have to protect them because of our pride."

"Will the white men come to Weinshauks?" John asked.

"Yes, unless they find the young man at Manisses. We shall protect him if he comes here. It is the law of the Pequotoog that one of our people must be judged by our king and executed by him or at his orders. If one Pequot kills another he shall either pay a blood price, if it will be accepted by the slain man's clan, or be executed by the sachem's tomahawk. The wonnux are now our sworn enemies. We cannot deliver him to be hanged at the end of a rope."

"It is a sad way to finish a feast, muckachuck," Wegun said. "Try to get some sleep so those great claw marks on your back will heal. Tomorrow the news may be better."

Early the next day, when John was finishing his morning meal, he heard a stir in the village. Several of the boys ran past the open doorway toward the gate which faced Pequot River.

He got to his feet and limped out to follow the Indians hurrying toward the west. He saw a young man coming up the hill from the waterfront. He was scratched and dirty, but he walked proudly. Mononotto met him at the gate.

"Greetings, Momoho," the sachem said. "Do you bring news from Manisses?"

"I do," the young sanop said, "and it is bad."

"Tell it," demanded Mononotto.

"The wonnux came to Manisses in their winged canoes. Their braves landed on the sandy shore. They were dressed for war in their shining coats and crests. One of our sanops shot an arrow at their sachem. It struck fairly on the crest and flew into the air without doing harm. A shower of our arrows struck the shining coats. Some broke in pieces. We knew we could not stand against their magic."

"Then what?" asked the sachem.

"We hid from them. There are many secret places on Manisses. The squaws and children had already found shelter among the dunes and beach-plum bushes. Our trails are hidden from the whites.

"But they did much harm to our two villages. They killed one sanop, burned our lodges, cut down the green corn and stole many fine mats and baskets. They chopped seven of our canoes into pieces. All of our store of dried corn and berries was taken or trampled into the ground."

"It is well that you brought this news," the sachem said. "Now that they have killed a sanop and burned the villages they may leave us in peace. Who sent you?"

"No one sent me. I came to find a hiding place."

"Why must you hide?"

"This is the reason," Momoho said. He raised a partly dried scalp stretched on a hoop.

"It is wonnux hair!" Mononotto exclaimed. "Were you the one who escaped from the great canoe?"

93

"Yes. I slew the white captain and took this." He waved the trophy before him. "When the other winged canoe attacked us I jumped overboard and swam to the shore. I was too strong for the magic of their bushkeagun."

"You did wrong to attack the canoe of the wonnux," Mononotto said, "but the greater evil was to come here for a hiding place. Now they will demand that we give you up. If we do not, they will kill and destroy here at Weinshauks as they did at Manisses."

"Momoho did the right thing in coming here. He shall have a place of refuge. I, Sassacus, have said it!"

John looked up to see the king standing in the gateway. Sassacus was dusty from his journey. The white boy could see a strong resemblance to his brothers, Kithansh, Tassaquanot, and Puppompogs, but hatred for the whites had lined his face into a savage scowl.

"It was not murder when Momoho slew the white captain," the king continued. "He killed an enemy. All wonnux are our enemies. They must be destroyed."

"Captain Oldham was a peaceful trader," Mononotto said.

"They all say they are peaceful," shouted Sassacus. He clutched his ceremonial tomahawk and jerked it up and down with short strokes. "It was at a peaceful trading post that they slew my father, without cause. They have taken our hunting grounds. Each day they cut and burn more trees and brush that used to shelter our game. Now they demand the lives of our young men."

He walked over to the Indian from Manisses and placed his hand on the young man's shoulder. "Momoho shall live to take many more scalps in the war that is to come. Are we

94

squaws to sit by and let them take him to hang on a rope and die? Are we afraid that the wonnux will hurt us?" He spat in the dust.

"It was not the English tribe of the wonnux who slew your father, but a tribe called the 'Dutch,'" Mononotto said.

"It matters not what name they call themselves, they are all wonnux, and the smell of the whites stinks in my nostrils. Who are they, that they should take our land and then spit on us? They ask for war—let it come!" Sassacus snarled.

"There should be some other way than war," the sachem said.

"Has the great Mononotto turned coward?" Sassacus demanded. He turned to look at him with eyes like slits. "Shall we dress him up in squaw's clothes so that he may sit in safety of his lodge? Even our women have more spirit than that."

"No one but my king can say that and live!" Mononotto replied in a steady voice. He reached for his knife. He was tense as he swung around toward Sassacus. "No man now living has ever doubted my courage. Withdraw your words or I shall forget your royalty! Grief has made you forget that our king rules with a council of his nobles. When that council says, 'Go on the warpath,' I shall lead."

"When the wonnux take the warpath I shall call that council. Until then I expect you to be loyal." Sassacus set his jaw and looked at his sachem.

"I am loyal to the Pequotoog, not to any one man," Mononotto replied as his hand dropped from the knife at his belt. "If any Pequot betrays my people, be he king, noble, or sanop, I shall be the first to ask the council to order him to turn his knife against his own heart."

The two nobles glared at each other. Then Mononotto walked over and extended his hand, palm down. "It is not well for Pequot to stand against Pequot," he said. "It was not my chief who spoke, but a son made mad by grief."

"It was well spoken, Mononotto," Sassacus said as he put his hand on that of the sachem. "It *is* a grieving son, but also a Pequot who knows that loss of pride will destroy the nation sooner than the guns of the English."

"They will come to seek Momoho," Mononotto said. "Are we to meet them at the shore?"

"Permit no white man to talk to one of our sachems. Select a sanop who can speak in a double tongue, saying one thing and meaning another." Sassacus looked at the sachem with a flicker of a smile. "Prepare for anything short of war. Send to the little village on the shore of the Pequotoog River and tell the squaws to carry that which is of value to the woods. If the wonnux come to Weinshauks we must be prepared to defend our homes—that is not war to be called by the council."

"It shall be done," Mononotto replied.

When he returned to the lodge, he looked out to see Momoho strutting by, swinging the partly dried scalp by a thong. Several of the young men of the village stopped to admire his trophy.

"It is such as he that brings our people to war," Wegun said. "Always the hotheads who call names or do things our older sanops are too wise to do. Then our pride makes us defend them."

"Pride and revenge," Mononotto said. "Revenge that makes the king strike out blindly against all white people. Pride that makes us hated by both red men and whites."

Before the sun was high, the next day, John saw small groups of armed sanops go down to the shore toward the huts. One of the bands came from the nearby fort at Mystic harbor.

During the afternoon the boys were shooting at a mark with their arrows. When John stood up to draw his bow, the boys shouted their encouragement. "It is Wahsus. Shoot straight or he will claw you!" called Cujep.

"When I shoot it is to kill the wonnux!" yelled Cocheat. The boys looked toward John and were silent.

He was hurt for a moment, then he realized how completely he had been accepted once more. The boys did not mention killing whites again, when he was around.

Bopoose grabbed John by the arm and swung him around. "Look, Cheegut! Do you see smoke rising over the trees?"

All of the boys stopped to gaze at the gray mist that rose in the direction of the river. Soon it became a column which grew larger and larger.

"That's the camping place where the squaws stay when they are digging and drying quahaugs," Duksors said. "Our sanops use it when they hunt ducks and geese." John was silent.

Some of the boys wanted to run to the shore until Cocheat said, "There may be a fight. Don't go there. Our sanops will send us back. Stay here and watch."

After a time the smoke died out and the boys walked back to the village. Squaws were dragging small trees into position around the palisade. Their stiff branches stabbed out from the upright logs. The boys found a narrow path leading to the gateway and filed through. Several sanops watched from the opening. One of them grunted and motioned for the boys to hurry through.

When John reached Wegun's lodge, he found her sitting with a half-finished basket before her. She did not speak. He squatted on the floor in silence. He had never seen her still for so long, and she never had failed to greet him.

There was a stir outside and a messenger arrived at the door of the lodge. "I seek Mononotto," he said.

"I shall send for him." Wegun dipped fresh water from a bucket and offered the gourd to the sanop. "Seat yourself, and drink. Cheegut will get the sachem."

The brave arose as Mononotto came in. "I bring word of the camping place," he said. "It is no more. The wonnux have come!"

"Tell me all that has happened," Mononotto said.

"The white people came in seven great winged canoes," the sanop said. "They wore armor and carried long knives, guns, and lances with shining points or steel ax heads on them. They stayed in their canoes while some of our people paddled out to meet them."

"Were they greeted as Sassacus ordered?"

"They were. No sachem was there. We wouldn't honor them by having a noble go to speak. Those who remained on the shore hid themselves in the bushes.

"We called to the English in their own tongue, 'What cheer, Netop.' That is what the Narragansetts' white father taught them to say. Then our spokesman, Messatunck, said, 'Where you come? What you look for?'

"The white sachem replied and Cutshamakin, of the Massachusetts, said after him in our tongue, 'We come from Boston and we seek your king, Sassacus.'

"Then Messatunck said, 'Sassacus far away. Him on Long Island. Much time for him to come. We call.'"

"Did the wonnux believe this?" Mononotto asked.

"They did, for a time. We paddled to the shore and pulled up our canoes far away from the magic of their guns. Then we came back where we could watch them and hear them talk. We laughed when we thought of all those whites waiting for a king who would never come." He took a sip of the water and wiped his lips with the back of his hand.

"Soon they tired from the long wait. Cutshamakin called to us, 'Where is Sassacus? You promised to bring him.'

"Messatunck shouted back, in their language, 'You angry with Pequotoog? You want to hurt?' The young men ran up and down the shore trying to shout the same words. They nearly fell down on the bank with weakness, laughing at the sound, and at the hairy, red-faced wonnux."

"Was it wise to taunt the enemy?" Mononotto said.

"It is always wise, O Sachem. The enemy then knows we do not fear him. They become so angry they do not shoot straight." He paused for a moment. "Their sachem stood forward and said through the Massachusetts, 'I demand to see Sassacus. We have waited too long.'

"Messatunck replied in our own tongue, 'Our king is much too great a man to come when such as you call. Why should he talk to the wonnux? Speak what you have to say to me, or go away.'

"This made the whites angry, as it was meant to do. They hauled up their anchors and drove the bows of their great canoes on the sandy beach. We shot arrows at them as they climbed the bank, but that did not stop them. Then we ran for the woods and thick brush to get away from the guns and long knives that swing and stab."

"It was then that they burned the huts?" Mononotto asked.

"Yes. They cut the corn that was ready to pick and carried it away. They took all of the mats and baskets that were good and spoiled the berries and quahaugs that had been dried and hidden in pits. There is nothing left but smoking ashes and a field of stripped cornstalks."

"Did any of the wonnux remain?"

"They have gone. Our sanops waited until they left the harbor. As they were going, one of them called out that they would never give up until they had taken Momoho."

When the messenger finished, he left the lodge. Mononotto looked toward Wegun but kept silent.

"It is a bad thing that has happened," she said. "Now a fire has been kindled, and no one knows how far it will burn."

Chapter Eight

OUTLAWS

KITHANSH was free for a short time after working on the defenses of the fort. He met John near Guldooke.

"We were nearly ready to have the purification and initiation that would make you a Pequot," he said. "After the bad news from Manisses and the attack on our huts, every thought has been the defense of Weinshauks."

"I was afraid the Pequotoog would turn against me," John replied. "Sassacus hates all whites and he shows his feelings whenever he sees me. There must be others who feel the same."

"Most of us forget your white blood. You have acted as a red man," Kithansh said. "There may yet be time for the ceremony."

"I cannot become a Pequot and fight against my own people," John said.

"If you are made a Pequot you will be washed clean of all white blood, you will be all Pequot," the young sanop replied. "But we do not wish to have you fight the whites. There are many enemies of ours who are red men. You can kill, scalp, or strike at a red foe in battle and win great fame."

John shook his head as he walked away. "I don't want

to be a sanop to kill and scalp," he told Wegun. "There must be some other way to serve."

Many times John saw the Indians look his way and motion as they talked. As he approached, they would stop abruptly and look off into space until he had passed.

"Of course they know you are different," Wegun told him. "They speak about you for several reasons. They know you do not wish to kill your own people. They fear that the white people will come to take you back by force. When they stop talking, it is because they do not want to offend you with the bitterness they feel to all other whites."

That afternoon an old sanop said to John, "Come with me, Cheegut, I will show you the work of a Pequot brave."

They walked together to the shore, a distance above the ruined huts. John saw a large number of the older men working in groups. Smoke from several small fires rose in the air. He could smell the odor of scorching wood.

"The Pequotoog have need for many war canoes. We have two harbors and much water in which to travel if we wish to defend our country. These are being built so that all of our sanops will have places when we travel." He motioned to several straight trunks of the tulip poplar, propped up clear of the ground. The bark had been removed and the ends of the great logs were plastered over with paint. This was dry and cracked as if it had been put on long ago.

"These have been cut for several winters," the old sanop said. "Now they are dry enough for our purpose. They come from far up the Pequot River and the river Quonnihticut. We floated them down in the high waters of spring. It was great labor to lift these clear of the ground, but it had to be done or the logs would have rotted. The bark was chopped away to save the wood from insects."

"Why do you paint the ends?" John asked.

"We do that to keep the logs from cracking, as they would if the ends dried faster than the rest of the trunk."

He pointed toward a group in which Kithansh was working. "This is not usually the work for young, impatient men. Only a few of them, like Kithansh, have been chosen to do it. When they are older they will teach others, as we were taught. Watch but do not try to help. Now I must work at my task."

There were three of the canoes being prepared at the same time. Two of them had the hulls well shaped. The other was still in the rough state. John found that he could barely span the end with outstretched arms. He paced the length and found it to be twenty of his strides. *That must be almost sixty feet,* he thought, *nearly as large as the war canoe of Sassacus.*

There were several groups at work, each with a small fire fed with hardwood chips. A sanop would scoop up glowing coals with a wooden shovel and place them in a hollow which was forming in a canoe. While he tended the blaze, blowing on the embers to make them char the wood, others worked at the opposite end of the craft. They scraped with sharpened stones and sea-clam shells that had been ground to a sharp edge. As they removed the charred portions, islands of unburned wood were left, which others chopped away with hand adzes. These were heavy stones with a sharp edge which they held in their fists.

When they had chopped and scraped down to the unburned wood, they exchanged places with the burner, who would kindle a new fire where they had finished. Sometimes the burner would pour a trickle of water around the fire he had kindled, to keep it from spreading.

John watched Kithansh measuring the thickness of the hull with two curved sticks lashed together at the ends.

"We make it this thick," the sanop said as he showed John the space between the open ends. "We do not burn or scrape too far."

"Don't the men get impatient with this slow burning, chopping and scraping?" John asked.

Kithansh made quick, sure strokes with the sharp stone. He looked up and said, "Red men do not get impatient. They work carefully for many days, knowing that one bad stroke may spoil everything."

While the Pequots were busy with their boatbuilding, a messenger arrived in a bark canoe. He looked angry as he lifted his craft from the water to the high ground, and then set out for Weinshauks. The workers watched him until he was over the hill. Then one sanop turned to another and said, "He brings bad news." He resumed his scraping. "Soon we'll hear about it. Bad news travels fast."

In a short time Mononotto came to the top of the hill and called several of the sanops by name, including Kithansh. John started to go with him, but Mononotto waved him back. "Stay here," Kithansh said. "You'll hear about it soon enough."

That evening Wegun said very little until they had finished their meal. When they had put aside their bowls, she said, "The word which the messenger brought was very bad news for the Pequotoog. A sachem of the Massachusetts, called Cutshamakin, killed one of our sanops.

He sent the scalp to Canonicus of the Narragansetts."

"Does that mean war with the tribe of the Massachusetts?" John asked.

"It is far worse than that. Canonicus received the scalp and then sent it by official messenger to all the nearby tribes that have submitted to the Pequotoog in the past. It has gone to the Niantics, the Mohegans, the Nipmucks and many others. All have received it and declared they will stand against us. We are alone, with all the red men joining the English."

"Is there any way we can win them back?" John asked, forgetting for the moment that he was not a Pequot.

"Sassacus and Mononotto, with several of our orators, are going to appeal to the tribes to stand together. They blame the white men for stirring up trouble between us. The Pequotoog hate the wonnux more than ever, now. The whites who live far from a fort will suffer."

That night a fire blazed near Guldooke. A large group of nobles and sanops sat in a circle about it. John crept near to the "good-luck tree" to hear what he could. He could see that the Indians were excited and angry.

"The wonnux are to blame for all of this," Sassacus said as he paced back and forth in front of his warriors. "We must win back the other red men and show them that the whites are not to be feared. We shall destroy until the hated wonnux fear the sound of our name and depart for their homes beyond the great water."

"Do we dance about Guldooke and send the snakeskin with arrows to the whites?" one sanop said.

"We shall not honor them by declaring war," the king replied. "Why should we treat them as we would the red man? No, we drive away their beasts, burn their lodges, ruin their farms. We'll kill their men and take the squaws and children for slaves. All this we can do and no Pequot need die." He gathered his feathered cloak about him.

"Tomorrow we go to Canonicus," he continued. "We shall tell him that the red men must stand together if we wish to keep our lands and our liberty. We know that he has a treaty of the 'talking leaves' with the wonnux, but this must be broken or there will soon be no living space for any of our tribes. I have spoken."

Shortly after dawn, Sassacus, Mononotto, and three nobles left for Narragansett. They carried with them their feathered cloaks, paint jars with ceremonial colors, and belts of wampum.

John and Wegun watched from the doorway of the lodge.

"Why do they carry the belts of wampum?" John asked. "Do they expect to buy peace with so little?"

"No, Cheegut. The wampum is not to buy anything. It is a ceremonial gift. If Canonicus takes it and puts it beside him, all is well. If he refuses to touch it, he shows that he does not wish to be friendly. Then he will refuse to hear our people."

"Is there no way in which he can show that he will listen, even if he is not friendly? We know that he sent the scalp to all the tribes, but he may want to hear what our sachems have to say."

"If he is ready to listen, he will tell Sassacus to put the gift on the mat between them. Then they may talk for a long time. Each side will have a chance to say what it thinks without being interrupted. It may be many days before they decide anything."

That night a storm struck the village. The gale blew slabs of bark from lodges and tore the thatch from roofs. Rain soaked the interior and turned the earthen floors to mud. Sheets of water swept across the council grounds, leaving pools and flattened grass in their wake. Lightning flashed and the thunder made children hide under their bed robes. Then the storm moved away from them toward the east, and the land of the Narragansetts.

"Hobbamuck is angry with the Pequotoog," said an old squaw who had found refuge in Wegun's lodge. "He follows our sachems to the land of our enemies. Now the fire sputters. Someone thinks ill of us." She spat in the blaze but it still sputtered.

At last the storm passed and all was calm. The morning came with the sun shining on pools of water and tangled wreckage. Branches torn from trees littered the ground. Gayly colored leaves were piled in bedraggled heaps against the lodges and the logs of the palisades. Squaws brought out blankets and bed mats to dry.

John walked along one of the paths from the main gate. He saw Kithansh taking charge of a working party of slaves. They were cutting logs and building barriers along the approach to the fort.

"Turn back, Cheegut!" Kithansh commanded. "Go back to the fort and stay there."

John turned and walked slowly toward the gateway. Then he was glad he had been sent back, because he found Wegun looking for him.

"Come to the lodge," she said. "I have great need for someone I can trust."

"I'm glad there is someone who trusts me," John said. "I've just been sent away from the outer works by Kithansh."

"These are bad times," Wegun said. "We can take no chances. But the mission I have for you is one I cannot trust to any Pequot. I have a message that must reach Mononotto at once. It is for his ears alone. Will you carry this word over those miles of trail?"

"I will go. The sanops have described the way. They spoke of the markings that messengers use when following it. If I start at once I can get there before the sun rises tomorrow."

"I know that you can travel far and fast," Wegun said. "You did that once, to my sorrow."

"Will they think I am running away once more?" John asked. "Can I have something to show that I am carrying a message?"

Wegun thought for a moment. Then she said, "Here, take my headband to show anyone who stops you. All the Pequotoog will know it and so will many of the Narragansetts." She handed him the narrow strip, woven with tiny purple and white beads.

John took it and, folding it, he stowed it in the deerskin pouch.

"It is the badge of a Narragansett princess," she said. "No other may wear it. The beads are the smallest that can be made from the shell of the quahaug. The weaving was done by the most skillful worker of the royal household. Guard it. There is no other like it.

"Tell Mononotto," she continued, "that one of his group, Wequash, has sold himself to the English. He is angry

108

because Sassacus chose Kithansh to command a division of sanops. He felt that he, as a noble and councilor, should have had that honor. I found out what he was going to do, but I have no proof that the Pequotoog will accept. Tell Mononotto to watch for treachery at the council of the Narragansetts. He will know that he must not accuse Wequash openly. We would lose his whole clan, the Swans."

"I'll start at once," John said. "It is not yet noon and I can reach the Niantic fort before the moon rises."

Wegun filled a bowl with steaming porridge. "Take and eat. I will pack dried food for your journey."

As John left the lodge, Wegun said, "Remember the message. Let no one but Mononotto hear you give it. When you have done this, seek out my mother. She will care for you until you return with the sachems."

John had to show the token several times before he was able to pass the barricades and reach the open trail.

The air was cool. Leaves that remained on the trees, after the gale, glowed red and gold in the sunshine. The brush was still wet, and pools of water had settled in spots. John's moccasined feet scuffed through masses of fallen leaves. Sometimes he slipped in wet clay.

At Mystic fort a sanop stopped him. "Where do you go, young bear killer, that you are in such a hurry? Do you run away once more?"

"I go on an errand for Wegun. Here is her token to show that she has sent me. I must reach Ninigret before dark."

"Yes. That is Wegun's badge," said the sanop. "You will have to make speed if you are to get to Ninigret by sundown. Now be careful of the 'little people' who live underground. They'll creep out after dark and steal that good knife of yours." He laughed when he saw that John was not frightened.

The water is too cold to swim across the harbor, John thought. *I'll have to go around the bay and wade across. I must run faster to make up time.*

The sun was halfway to the horizon when he forded the Pawcatuck River. *Now it is over two hours to Ninigret, but I'm in Niantic country. They guard the approaches to the Narragansett country and I may be challenged any moment.*

The sun set in a blaze of red and orange. It sent a broad path of gold across the waters of the great sound to his right. A few scattered clouds held the color against the blue sky after the sun had disappeared. This afterglow was just fading when he sighted Fort Ninigret.

He walked slowly, expecting a challenge. It was not long before he heard a harsh voice shout from a nearby thicket, *"Tawhitch kuppeeyoumen!"*

John raised his right hand to show that he held no weapon, and answered, "I come to find the trail to Canonicus. I travel on royal business and cannot be stopped."

"No one passes to the fort of Canonicus tonight. You come from the direction of the Pequotoog. Too many of them have passed this way to please us. Are you a Pequot? Your speech does not have the sound of one."

"I come from Wegun with a message to one of her family," John answered. "I must travel fast."

"Wegun?" questioned the Niantic as he came into the open. He held his bow in readiness. "How do I know that you do not speak with a double tongue?"

"This is my proof," John said as he drew out the beaded strip. "She told me the Niantics would recognize the badge of a Narragansett princess."

The Niantic took the brow band in his hand. "This feels like fine beadwork," he said. "Come to the fort with me so I can examine it by the light of a torch. Who are you?"

"I am Wegun's muckachuck. She asked me to make speed so that I may reach her mother before it is too late."

"We have heard of you, bear killer. Come to the fort to eat and rest. The boys will be glad to hear of your fight."

"I have eaten and I am not tired. Let me pass at once. I cannot wait."

"Go your way, muckachuck. Watch the trail where it forks. Turn to the left. The right will lead to the landing place far from where you want to go. Be ready to answer quickly when you are challenged. The Narragansetts shoot or stab first before they spend too much time talking. You will be stopped many times. Here's your token—guard it well."

The brave vanished in the shadows and all was still. John trotted along the trail, seeing it dimly by the star-light, and feeling its firmness through the thin soles of his moccasins. When he reached the fork, he turned left. The ground was now rising in a succession of short, steep hills. A glow in the sky showed where the moon was about to rise.

He stopped at the top of one of the hills to get his breath. He was about to go on when a sharp voice called on him to halt. He felt the sharp point of a lance against the bare flesh of his stomach. "Who goes this way in the dark?"

the voice said. "Those who have business with the Narragansetts travel by daylight so they may be seen."

"I am Wegun's messenger," replied John. "I do not come creeping like a shkook. I come running in the open. I must reach the council house tonight."

"Wegun deserves better than to have to live as a Pequot. Who are you? Your language has a strange sound."

"I am named Cheegut. I have lived in Wegun's lodge for many moons."

"You are a white boy!" the brave said as he felt of the boy's hair and examined his face in the light of the moon. "How do I know she sent you?"

"This is her token," John said as he handed the band to the sentry.

The Narragansett held it close to his eyes and felt of its texture. "This is truly Wegun's. My mother wove it for her to take into the land of the Pequotoog so that she would always remember that she was a Narragansett princess. Come with me. I will show you the way to Canonicus' fort. When you get there you will have to answer why you came in such haste."

He called softly, and another sentry appeared as silently as a shadow. "Stand guard while I go with this young messenger," he said. Then he signaled John to follow.

All along the trail John was aware of guards. His guide would give the call of the screech owl, a soft, eerie sound, and a dim figure would appear and then blend into the shadow of bush or tree.

When they came to the palisaded fort, his guide led him through the narrow gateway without being challenged. There was a great circle of lodges and a long house in the

112

center. John could see the glow of a fire inside and heard a speaker. Torches smoked and flickered at intervals around this lodge, and armed sentries stood guard.

"You said you wanted to go to the council house," his guide said. "Did you mean the house of Wegun's mother?" He pointed to one of the larger structures.

"My message is for Mononotto, Wegun's husband. There is no time to be lost."

The guide turned to him and scowled. "You come with a message for a Pequot sachem—here at our great council?"

"It is a message from a Narragansett princess," John replied. "I must see Mononotto at once."

The guide grunted, then turned to the doorway of the council house and spoke to the guard. He turned to John and said, "Let this sentry take the token to the Pequot so that he may know who calls him."

In a few minutes Mononotto appeared. "Has something happened to Wegun that she sends you in such haste? Speak up, Cheegut!"

"I must speak where no one but you can hear," John said. "Wegun is safe and well. This is about the great mission and I have been traveling since noon today."

"You did well," Mononotto replied as they walked a short distance from the entrance and the ring of guards. "Now tell me why you were sent."

When John told him of Wegun's suspicion and the need for caution in acting against Wequash, because of his clan, the sachem nodded. "She did well to warn me, and secretly. Wequash has already done harm. I thought he had blundered, but now all is clear. I shall handle this myself, as Sassacus would sink his tomahawk in the traitor's skull.

He would not stop to think of its being the Narragansett council house, nor of the loss of the Swan Clan. You have done well, Cheegut. In every way you have acted as my son."

"I'm sorry I didn't get here sooner. You might have prevented his speaking in the council," John said.

"It was not there but about the village," Mononotto said. "He boasted that we did not need the Narragansett help. He told them the Pequotoog would punish those who were friendly to the wonnux. Now I can see that he meant to defeat our mission here."

Mononotto listened to the sound of voices from the council house and turned to John, "Would you like to hear the 'white father' of the Narragansetts? He is starting to speak and all will listen. Creep in when I go. Stay back near the wall and make no sound. Come."

John found a place near the wall where he could see and hear the speakers. There were few Indians near him. He could see the backs of those on one side of the oval about the central fire and the glint of firelight in the eyes of those on the opposite side.

At the end of the oval was a pile of mats with two sachems reclining on them. One was old and wrinkled. The other was a young man.

Then he was aware that the person who was speaking was not an Indian. He was tall, but not so tall as his slight figure made one think. He was dressed in knee breeches with stockings and square-toed shoes with shining buckles. *He must be a minister*, John thought. *He has a white collar and tabs just like the minister at Watertown. And the same kind of coat buttoned up to his throat.* Then he

114

remembered that Mononotto had said the "white father" was to speak. *It must be Roger Williams.*

The speaker had made his greeting to the rulers. Now he turned first to one side and then the other of the group about the fire. His dark hair hung almost to his shoulders and it seemed to be constantly in motion as he spoke. His voice came back to John distinctly, yet it did not seem to be loud. He was speaking in the Narragansett tongue, which was like the Pequot except for slight differences in pronunciation.

His Indian listeners were almost motionless. Occasionally a Narragansett would nod his head. Over near the sachem were the Pequot nobles. John thought they looked worried.

"The red men have laws that give justice to those in the tribe. If one steals from another he must return twofold. If he kills another your laws demand that he give his life. The sachem's tomahawk carries out this sentence.

"The white men have the same laws for justice. These protect the lives and the goods of the colony.

"The 'talking leaves' show us how red men and white can live together if all will heed them. If a white man slays an Indian he is judged by the white man's court and his life is taken. So let it be if one of your people kills a white person.

"Peace cannot be kept if the murderer of the white captain remains unpunished. Give him up to justice and the white men will know that you desire to live at peace with them. Then they will believe that you and the rest of the great Algonquin people wish to be friends. From the Abnaki in the north to the Leni Lenápe in the south and from the great water to the land of the Five Nations, the Iroquois, the red men and the whites will be able to live together without fear."

Then he turned to the two sachems, seated on the mats, and said, "I appeal to the wise king, Canonicus, known for generations as just. I appeal to the young king, Miantonomo, who rules with him and administers this justice. If a sanop offends he is punished. Should not a nation of the great brotherhood of red men be punished if it defies the law?"

Roger Williams stood for a moment as he looked about him. Then he said, "I have finished."

He sat down on a mat near the sachems. There was a hum of voices and angry words from several of the Pequotoog. Then Sassacus rose and signaled that he wished to speak. Canonicus nodded to him and motioned for silence.

"The white father has told you of the treaty which Miantonomo made with the English. While the Narragansetts feasted and had much talk with them no one thought to invite the Pequotoog. Is that justice to condemn a nation unheard? When the talking leaves were sent to the Narragansetts none were sent to the Pequotoog. Your treaty was an invitation to make war on your red brothers and not a plan for peace. The white father has not told you of the many evils which will follow.

"The talking leaves tell you to destroy our nation and be friends with these strangers from across the great water. It says to kill our young men or take them captive to be sent to the wonnux for punishment. What evil is this that turns you against your own kind?

"I see many who shake their heads. It is true that the

hands of the Pequotoog have been turned against other tribes. So it has been with the Narragansetts. Consider the Niantics to the west, the Cowesets, the Shawomets, and the Nipmucks to the north. Then there are the island tribes to the east. All of these pay tribute to the Narragansetts. Are the Pequotoog so evil because they have done this to a few?"

Sassacus turned to Roger Williams. "Did not the English, with their Captain Standish, make the people of the proud Narragansetts humble? Do they remember the arrows and snakeskin that they sent to Plymouth? Did not Standish return this skin filled with magic sand and bullets, which all feared to touch? Do the Narragansetts love the wonnux more because they shamed them?

"These English are strangers. Their blood is different." He held out his arms as if to show the difference. Then, spreading them wide, he said in a soft voice, "If there are quarrels in a family they are soon forgotten if strangers interfere. So let it be with red brothers."

Sassacus paced back and forth, as if in thought. "We are told that the wonnux have many brothers in their far land. If they find that they can work their will in this country of ours, they will swarm like locusts to eat us up. These are our lands." He stretched his right arm and swung it in a complete circle as he turned. "This has been the country of the red man from ancient times. Are we to be driven from it to become wanderers? Are we to have no place to hunt, or fish, or breathe free air?"

Then his voice became so loud that it beat on John's ears. "Let us join forces. United we shall be as a great waterfall that no man can stop. We do not need to face shining coats and guns in open battle. We can fire their homes, kill their cattle, destroy from ambush until their blood becomes as water. Then they will flee to their homes across the great water and never return."

He turned to the white-haired king and lowered his voice. "I call upon your wisdom of eighty winters, O Canonicus, to see that what I speak is the truth. I have spoken."

As Sassacus sat down there was a murmur among the Narragansetts. One of the younger sanops started to rise, but older warriors pulled him back to his seat.

Roger Williams sprang to his feet and looked toward the king. Canonicus signaled to him that he might speak.

"Is this the price the Pequotoog demanded of the proud Niantics to buy peace?" He reached for one of the belts of wampum and held it high above his head. Then he picked another and held the two of them high above his head. "Is this the price? No! The price was many times this. It was their food, their blankets, their young men to labor as slaves, and their pride. Each spring one Pequot brave comes to Ninigret for tribute. Each spring the demand is greater than the last as Niantic warriors stagger out with this booty to carry it to their masters. Three thousand Niantic sanops tremble and lose their manhood before one Pequot warrior.

"This is true of many other nations that have felt the heavy hand of the Destroyers. There will be no relief until you are freed from slavery and the fear of destruction.

"When the evil spirit struck the red men with sickness and death, who came to feed and nurse you? Who taught you better ways of life? Who has been willing to share with you the love of the Great Spirit? Are these the people that Sassacus says will eat you up?

"Of your own free will, guided by the wisdom of your two kings, the Narragansetts have made a treaty with the English at Boston. It promises peace between the people from father to son. Is that treaty of less value because the Pequotoog sit there scowling and fingering their tomahawks? No! It is more greatly needed."

Roger Williams laid the belts on the mat and turned to the circle of Narragansetts. "When we greet you as *netop*, that is what we mean, you are our friend. The 'Great Father' made us brothers and we should be friends." Then he faced the rulers and said, "I have spoken."

"The hour is late," said Canonicus. "We have put these gifts of the Pequotoog on the mat before us. We shall not accept or refuse them until we have called upon Kiehtan to guide us, as the white man is guided by his Great Spirit. Do nothing in anger and nothing in fear. Go in peace and return tomorrow."

The council broke up with excited talk and some angry words. John rejoined Mononotto, who said, "The Pequotoog have had their own way so long that they have made many enemies. We have driven away many of our own nation. Uncas was once a sachem of the Pequotoog. He was driven away in anger and in jealousy. Now he is a sachem of the Mohegans. Wequash is another who might have been saved by fair treatment. How can we expect the English and Narragansetts to trust us when we cannot hold the loyalty of our own people?

"Now it is time for you to go to the lodge of Wegun's mother. It is late and you have come a long way." The sachem led John through the dark cluster of wigwams to one that was larger than those about it. He motioned to the boy to follow him and then he stepped into the doorway without knocking.

"This is Cheegut," said Mononotto. "He is Wegun's muckachuck and mine too. You asked to have him stay with you so here he is." The sachem pushed John toward the old woman and then backed out through the doorway.

"You will sleep there," said the old woman. "Tomorrow I must hear about my daughter."

John was asleep as soon as he closed his eyes and did not awaken until morning.

"How is Wegun?" said her mother. "Is she well? And what of Nemud? You are almost my grandson too."

John told her the news of Weinshauks as she sat on a pile of mats. Her eyes were bright and her back straight as she listened.

She was old. Her white hair was drawn away from her wrinkled forehead and held by a beaded band. John saw that it had the same designs as Wegun's.

"Mononotto tells me that you ran from Weinshauks to our council house with word from my daughter. He says you traveled faster than most of the messengers. He is proud of you."

"I am pleased that he is," John said. "He has been good to me. Last night he found a way to get me into the council house. I heard Roger Williams speak."

"The white father is the Narragansetts' best friend. He has been ready to help us when we were in need. He tells us he is repaying the red men for their kindness to him."

"Tell me about him," John said.

"Many winters ago, when the snow lay deep and the trees cracked with the cold, a white man came to Canonicus and sought shelter. He was a powow of the English, but he had offended them. They wished to put him in a winged canoe to be sent across the great water. There he would have been killed or put in prison. He escaped and traveled many miles through snow and ice to find refuge with the red men.

"The Narragansetts sold him land on the river Seekonk. He named his place 'Providence' and said that all who were in trouble could come there.

"He has helped the red men, because of their kindness. His counsel is wise. He has taught them how to make their life easier. He is the only one among us who can read the talking leaves and he makes them speak in our language. He heals the sick, not as our powows do, but he is careful not to offend them."

"How did he happen to be here at this time?" John asked.

"When the Pequotoog first came to the council, Sassacus talked much about destroying all white people. Canonicus has sworn to stand by his English friends but he feared the strength of the Destroyers. He sent a message to the white father to come and speak in council. In the tempest, two nights ago when Hobbamuck showed his anger, the white man paddled alone in a bark canoe and came here wet and cold. He said that the Great Spirit had brought him in safety. It must be so.

"He dried his clothes before the fire, put on a white collar from his pack. He went to the council just as our young men were shouting, 'Burn the treaty with the

English! Kill! Destroy!' "

The next day John met Roger Williams, who greeted him with the English salutation, "What cheer, netop?" Then he continued in the Pequot tongue, "I see by your clothes that you are a Pequot boy. Is your father one of the nobles who spoke in council?"

"I live with Mononotto," John replied. "He is a sachem." He spoke in Pequot, hoping that Williams would not discover he was English.

The white father looked at him closely. With a gentle hand, he took John's chin and turned his face up to him. "You are a white boy!" he exclaimed. "How did you get here?"

John pulled away from him.

"Have no fear. If you wish help, I can give it to you. If you desire to be let alone, I can promise that, too."

"If the help you give me will return me to the English, I do not wish it," John replied. "My Indian parents are in trouble and I must stay with them to help. My own are dead and I was bound to Master Hoskins. If I return, it will be to be punished and enslaved once more."

"Our treaty says we must return all runaway servants to their masters, but I promised to let you alone if you wished. Why did you go to the Pequots?"

John told him of his capture and his attempt to rejoin his guardian at Wethersfield. "Mononotto and Wegun have been good to me. Now that they are in trouble I cannot leave them. You could help by not speaking so strongly against my people."

"That is the hardest part of my mission, my son. The innocent must suffer with the guilty. If troubles come too heavily for you to bear, I can offer you and your friends a new home and peace in Providence. Remember that when you hear that I have been too severe with the men of the Pequotoog who have broken the laws of God and man." He smiled at John and went toward the council house.

Late that day, Mononotto came into the lodge and put down the wampum belts. "It is finished," he said. "They have refused to accept the gift. They will stand by their treaty with the English. It was the white father who held them with his talk, but I cannot find it in my heart to hate him. Sassacus refuses to give up Momoho. We leave at sunrise as enemies and outlaws."

"Can we get away?" John asked.

"We can. Canonicus and Miantonomo have promised safe-conduct as far as our border on the Pawcatuck river. After that every hand will be against us. Do you wish to stay with Wegun's mother? I think that is as Wegun wishes it."

"I will go with you," John replied. "All my friends are in Weinshauks and I will stay with them."

At dawn the four Pequots called for John. "Wequash is staying with the Narragansetts," Mononotto said. "He knows that we suspect him. On the last day of the council he stood and spoke against us. There is no return for him."

"Wequash is a name we shall no longer speak!" Sassacus said. "He is a traitor and his clan of the Swan shall suffer!"

"They are too strong to punish without weakening our nation," Mononotto said. "We must watch them."

A strong party of Narragansetts kept near the Pequots all the way to Ninigret. There they were met by the

Niantics, who marched with their allies as far as the river. They jeered and threatened the Pequots with torture and death. As they neared the border, John noticed that they dropped farther and farther to the rear. They were out of sight when the Pequots waded the river to their own territory.

When they entered Weinshauks, the people received the news and moved away in silence.

"We must be bold and do things that will show our people that we still have spirit," Sassacus said. "The Pequotoog have been strong and feared by others because we struck out as warriors. The wonnux and the traitor red men must be taught that we are still the Destroyers. Let there be sorrow among them that they have made us their enemies. After we drive away the whites, let us make the cowardly red men our slaves. Our nation will be greater than before."

"Kill and destroy!" said one of the sanops as he drew his tomahawk and felt its edge. "The white father truly said that one Pequot brave could make three thousand Niantics tremble. We'll strike and make all wonnux fear. Then we'll drive them across the great water. When they're gone we'll eat up the Narragansetts and all their friends."

"We'll raid the settlements along the great river," Sassacus said. "When we have their guns and the magic sand no one can stop us."

"They have not seen what I've seen," said Mommenoteck. "The English will come from across the great waters and sweep all red men from their lands. They are numbered as the sand on the beach."

Chapter Nine

THE RAID

"Hunting has been poor this fall," Kithansh said. "Now that winter is starting we can find no game. If it snows we may be able to see the tracks."

"Do you hunt in the winter with bow and arrow?" John asked.

"We do, but mostly with traps. We place them where we see the runs in the snow. Mononotto says you can go with us if you wish. You are a good shot with the bow."

"I want to go. When do we start?"

"Tomorrow. Bring your weapons, dry food, and a blanket. Be sure to dress warmly."

The sky was overcast the next morning. The chill penetrated John's clothes. He wore his hunting shirt, leggings, and moccasins. Over his shoulders he had a cape of beaver with the fur inside. He drew this about him as he waited for the sanops to appear.

He felt that he had done well in preparing for the trip. He had oiled his bow the night before and selected straight arrows to fill his quiver. Wegun had put food in his pouch. She had selected a wool blanket and an extra shirt to roll in the deerskin pack.

"We go away together this time," said Wunx as he joined the boy. "Here comes Wahsus."

125

Kithansh completed the party. As he came up he said, "It will snow soon. That will be good for tracking."

During the morning the snow started. There were a few fine feathers of it at first. In the stillness of the woods John could hear the gentle rustle of the flakes as they fell through the dry oak leaves that clung to the trees. Soon there was a light powdering of white on the ground. All of them looked for signs of game.

It was not until they reached the border of the Mohegan country that they found any signs of life. Here they saw the paw prints of a wolf and one place where it had made its kill.

"We camp here tonight," Kithansh said. "Then we can look about in the morning. If the wolves can find food, so can we."

They picked a sheltered spot in a hollow and worked together to make a hut of branches. They covered the frame with dry sod and packed earth, leaving a hole in the roof for smoke. When it was finished they built a small fire in the center and the four of them crawled in to sleep.

All the next day they set traps along the paths that deer and smaller animals might travel. Kithansh showed him how to set the snares and how to make the heavy stone dead falls that would kill any wolf that might try to rob the trap.

For several days they caught barely enough to feed themselves. Then they moved their camp another day's journey. The Pequots moved cautiously. "We watch for Mohegans as well as game," said Wunx.

They found animals in a few of their traps. What flesh they didn't eat they cut in thin strips to dry over the fire.

They were away from Weinshauks nearly a month and their packs of meat were still small. John was now traveling farther away by himself. Kithansh warned, "Keep a sharp watch for Mohegans. They will kill any Pequot they find hunting in their country."

One day, as John was walking along the trap line, he heard a slight sound in the brush ahead of him. He stood very still. *Is it a Mohegan or some animal?* Then he saw a deer feeding on young twigs and buds. The wind was blowing in his direction and the deer continued to browse, without being alarmed. John moved very slowly as he kneeled and fitted an arrow to his string. He waited as the animal moved nearer, step by step. Then the boy took aim, held his breath, and loosed the shaft. He thought he could see it fly true to its mark. The deer leaped in the air and crashed through the brush to vanish from his sight.

John found the tracks. Then he saw a red stain. As he followed the tracks, the stains were larger, until ahead of him he saw the still form in the snow.

He drew his knife and held it in readiness, but did not need to use it.

He drew out the arrow and wiped it clean. Then he struggled to lift the body and found it too heavy to carry. *If I leave it here the wolves will find it before I can get help to carry it.*

He staggered along the trail, dragging the buck. He made slow progress because he tried to conceal the track he was making. Then he gave up trying and tugged at the heavy body. He was still far from their hut when he heard a harsh voice say, "What does a Pequot mean by hunting in the land of the Mohegans?"

An angry Indian came out of the thick brush. Behind him was another, who fingered his tomahawk. John dropped his load and straightened up. There was little chance to fight against these odds. *I'll face them and show them I am not afraid.* He knew there would be no mercy shown.

"We take the deer," said one Mohegan as he raised his tomahawk. "It is ours. You shall die!"

John dodged as the tomahawk whizzed past his head. Drawing his hunting knife he rushed at the Indian. He was astonished to see the Mohegan turn and run. The other Indian seemed to vanish. John could not believe that he had frightened two Mohegan braves. He turned when he heard a sound behind him, and saw Kithansh and his two companions coming toward him.

"Well done, Cheegut!" the young sachem shouted as he clapped John on the shoulder. "You might have returned with an enemy scalp. That would be something to show at Weinshauks. A battle trophy before you are old enough to be a warrior!"

Wahsus had been searching in the bushes and he came out with the tomahawk that the Mohegan had thrown. "Take this," he said. "Everyone will recognize a Mohegan ax. What a prize to show the boys!"

They fastened the deer to a branch so the four of them could carry the body. "Now get away from the Mohegan country before those wolves carry word to their camp! The whole pack will be on our trail. Hurry! Get to the hut, cut up the meat so we can carry it, and get away to a place where we can dry and smoke it."

They skinned the deer and cut the meat. Wahsus was

the most skillful butcher, and John lent him his knife. At each stroke of the sharp steel Wahsus would say, "Good! Good!" When he finished, he handed the knife back to John and said, "No wonder you could kill a bear. The knife did it for you." He grinned as he said it.

"The fresh meat is a heavy load for a strong man to carry with the *muttoumbe*," said Kithansh. "It is too much for you, even if you did kill the deer."

It took three days to reach Weinshauks. The snow was deep in some places and they had to watch for Mohegans. At times John felt that his load was too much for him. The tumpline drew against his forehead and the load chafed his back. Every muscle seemed to be aching and his neck and jaws were stiff.

There was great excitement in Weinsauks when the braves told of John's adventure. The boys fingered the tomahawk. Duksors said, "It is almost as good as a scalp."

"It's better," Cujep said. "With this, Cheegut can get many scalps."

Other parties straggled in. Their packs were light and they said the hunting was poor wherever they went.

"In the days before this trouble," Wegun said. "We fished and dug quahaugs to dry and trade for smoked meat. Now we must live on the things we get from the streams and shores."

"It is red meat that is the red man's food," Mononotto said. "We have little of that, and only a small supply of corn. There will be hunger in Weinshauks and at the Mystic fort."

"We must divide the food that we have," said Sassacus. "Kithansh and Mononotto will take charge to see that no one gets more than his share each day."

John went to the coves with the boys to try for quahaugs and oysters until the shore ice piled so deep that it completely buried the shellfish. Under the snow, the ground was so glass-hard that they could get no roots. They returned to the village with young twigs and tree bark. Everything else was sealed in the grip of winter.

When early spring melted the snow and started the herring run there were empty lodges and squaws who were too weak to wail for their lost ones.

With the return of fish and game and the sprouting of small green things John began to think of the spring planting at the Hoskins' settlement.

"It has been almost a year since I last saw Wethersfield," John said to Wegun.

"Do you still want to go back?" she asked. "I hoped you would want to stay. But we have starved and suffered with the cold. I don't think we have the right to ask you to go through with what lies ahead. I have talked with Mononotto and others. They feel as I do, we should let you go back to the white men. The white father would see that you got back safely."

"I want to stay with you and Nemud," John said. "There is need for me here."

"When I sent you with that message to Mononotto, I thought you might stay with the Narragansetts. Mononotto did too. He asked you."

"I remember," John said, "but I felt like a stranger. They thought of me as either a Pequot or a white boy.

"Our troubles will be over when the English take Momoho," John continued.

"That is too much to hope for," Wegun replied. "Sassacus hates the wonnux. He can think of nothing but driving them away. The young men want to fight, to take scalps, to win honor." Wegun looked toward the dancing place, where a large band of sanops were gathered about Guldooke. "See, they are getting ready for a raid. Tassaquanot, the brother of Sassacus and Kithansh, is the leader."

"Where are they going?" John asked.

"They do not tell. Only the leader knows until they are on the trail. With so many, it may be along the valley of the great river. There are several large settlements there."

"The settlers there at Hartford, Windsor, and Wethersfield came in peace," John said. "They bought their land from the Wangunks and they have harmed nobody. Why should they be attacked?"

"It is because they are white, and Sassacus can't be changed. The small raids gave them a taste for the steel knives and axes. The household goods, kettles and pans, make the squaws eager to have them raid some more. They are glad to follow the king for the excitement and the wealth of such things.

"Sassacus has several of the white men's guns in his lodge, wrapped in mats. He waits for more of these and the knowledge of how to use them. He needs powder and bullets, too, and hopes to get prisoners who will tell how they are made. We do not know the magic."

"The guns are not magic," John said. "I was taught to load and shoot a musket, but I do not know how they make powder. They use regular molds in which they pour the hot lead when they make bullets."

"Our sanops are learning to lose their fear," Wegun

said. "Each day they lift the mats and handle the guns. They are not hurt by them, so they are becoming brave."

"Has Sassacus ever talked to Mommenoteck about the English who are over the great water?" said John.

"We have all heard this from the old sachem. He is so fearful that many call him 'old woman,' behind his back. He does not speak about it any more. There is no one who will listen."

"Our people at Wethersfield are plowing for spring planting," John said. "They will be away from their homes and unarmed. Even if they did get together with every man from the settlement, there would not be as many as Tassaquanot is taking."

"They have planned it this way," Wegun said. "After the Pequotoog have passed that way there will be smoking ruins and lifeless bodies. I dread the capture of prisoners. They take joy in torturing their captives. Sanops and squaws who are friendly now turn into savage animals."

"Do they torture and kill all of their captives?"

"No. Some are kept as slaves and a few are adopted."

Perhaps they are not going up the Connecticut river after all, John thought. *There are other settlements. I must stop thinking about it. There is nothing I can do.*

Time seemed to drag. The raiding party had been away for three days. John was with Bopoose and Duksors at the ruins along the shore. They sifted the ashes of the burned huts to find arrowheads or household pots. Squaws were digging in the sand and mud for long-necked clams. Several sanops were working on war canoes, rubbing grease into the hulls or smoothing rough spots.

"Look!" shouted Bopoose. "What is that far out in the sound?"

The sanops stopped their work and ran to where the boy stood, pointing.

"It is Tassaquanot and his party," said one. "Hi, Duksors! You are well named the 'Rabbit.' Run and tell those at Weinshauks what we have seen."

Duksors dashed off toward the fort. The sanops laughed to see him plunge along with his arms driving and his legs twinkling as they carried him over the hill.

"He will bring everybody in a hurry," said one. "It takes a boy to stir things up."

"He will not need to stir them up," said another. "There are many who will come to greet their own."

The canoes were now in plain sight. The long, narrow hulls drove through the water as flashing paddles rose and stroked in cadence. Soon they could hear the sound of the leaders calling the stroke.

Three war canoes were in the lead, and far behind a fourth one came on more slowly. By the time the boats had come up the Pequot River, Indians were running down to the shore. A sanop laughed as a fat squaw stumbled and fell. She was up in an instant and came puffing, and tripping over stones in her haste.

As soon as the three war canoes reached the shore, the paddlers jumped out and eased the hulls over the pebbles and shells. By the time they had lifted their boats high on the shore, the fourth one limped in. Its bow was shattered almost to the waterline. The paddlers kneeled well back to keep the hole above water.

John saw two white girls huddled in the center of the craft. They were trying to cover their near nakedness with torn clothing. He was so intent on this canoe that he hardly noticed the actions of the other raiders. When they came ashore they danced about, waving their arms and shouting. Many of them had dressed themselves in fantastic style. One sanop had a woman's sunbonnet perched on his bristly crest. Another had put on a woman's dress backward. All of them had articles of clothing, tools, and household utensils which they waved to friends on the bank.

"See where the wonnux shot at us with their big bushkeag from the fort!" shouted the paddler nearest the shattered bow. "There was a great noise and smoke as we passed. The stone bit a piece out of the canoe, but it never hurt us. Their magic is weak."

As the damaged canoe was drawn up on the narrow beach, the young sanops jumped out dragging the two girls after them. One of the children could not keep her feet and she was hauled across the pebbly beach like a limp sack. When the young men flung the girls down on dry land, the squaws rushed at them, screaming. They beat the two girls with sticks. One of them grabbed the older girl by the hair and dragged her toward the bank.

"Stop!" shouted Mononotto, who had just reached the scene. "Are you Wangunks that you let the squaws mistreat captive children? Drive the rabble away. Take the girls to my lodge."

The noise ceased. Squaws hurried away. Children stood by, wondering what would happen next. Mononotto seldom raised his voice in anger.

Tassaquanot stopped grinning and turned to his war party. "Take off the things and act like men," he said. They put the garments out of sight. It was then that John saw the bloody scalps and the bundle of muskets wrapped in a mat.

Two older warriors hustled the girls up the path to Weinshauks. John followed them through the gateway to the lodge.

"Why have you brought the white girls to this village?" Wegun asked as she stood in the doorway and looked at the group. "Have you brought these small ones for slaves? What kind of work can they do?"

"Mononotto said to take them to his lodge," said one sanop. "The squaws were treating them badly."

"It is well that you saved them from the squaws, but you haven't answered my question. Why were they taken prisoner? You know the wonnux will seek the girls to save them. They will not leave a lodge unburned or a red man alive until they find them. It is worse than if you had killed them."

"We brought them because of the bushkeagun," said the sanop. "We have five more of them. The girls will tell how to make them speak and how to make magic black sand."

"If you wished to have them tell you these things, why did you mistreat them?"

"We did it to make them fear us. Now they will tell so we will let them alone."

"I don't believe the wonnux teach their children such things. If they did, you have driven all knowledge from their heads."

"Torture will open their lips," blustered one of the braves.

"And show they are empty of knowledge," Wegun said. "Leave them with me. If they know anything they can tell it better after they have been quieted. Now go!"

The girls were sobbing. The older one moved her lips as if she were praying.

"Don't be afraid," John whispered in English. "Wegun is good. She will not let them hurt you any more." He looked about to see if anyone could overhear.

Both girls turned quickly. The older one said, "Who are you?"

"Speak softly. I am John Bishop. I stayed with William Hoskins near Wethersfield."

"You are the boy who ran away," she said. "I heard about you. Now I'm ashamed for you. You are one of these dreadful Pequots!"

"I did not run away. I was stolen and brought here. If you won't trust me I can't help you."

"I'm going to have to trust you," she whispered. "I'm Susan Swain and this is my sister Hepsy. My father is Abraham Swain. I fear he was killed when they attacked him in the field." She choked up and Hepsy sobbed. "I hope we can get back with white folks. Maybe we can find someone to take us in. I prayed every minute, and maybe you're the answer. You and the Indian woman."

"She is the wife of the sachem who stopped the squaws down at the shore. He is next to the king in greatness."

John looked about to see if anyone was watching. "We shall have to be careful," he whispered. "No one must see us talking together."

Chapter Ten

WAR!

SEVERAL days after the return of the raiding party, Mononotto brought a few of the nobles to the lodge. Several young sanops carried muskets and laid them on mats spread out on the floor.

"Are the young squaws calm enough to talk to us?" Mononotto asked Wegun. "If so, have them come here."

"They are no longer terrified," Wegun replied. "They hope to see their people soon. Do you plan to let them go?"

"We did not, at first," the sachem said. "They are strong and would make good slaves. Now things have changed. We can send them back and receive goods or wampum from the wonnux."

"I was afraid the white people would attack us after the raid on their village and the capture of the children. We are not yet ready for that."

"The English know that we would torture and kill these children if they came against us," Mononotto replied. "They sent word by the Dutch white men that they would pay ransom for these if they were returned unharmed."

"I'm glad you are going to send them back. Shall I prepare them? They'll need clothing of the whites, not the Pequot skirts they are wearing now."

"We are not ready yet. Not until they show us all they

know about the guns and powder."

"Then that will be soon," said Wegun, "because they know little or nothing about such things."

"They must be tortured until they tell," one old sanop said. "They must have seen their warriors make the magic sand and shoot the bushkeagun. A little suffering will make them remember."

"And it will bring the English here before we are ready," Mononotto said, turning to the old brave. "They hold back only as long as the children are unharmed. When we torture them the whites will come with their long knives and guns."

"How will they know what we do? Are they magicians, that they can see afar off?"

"All Pequots are not loyal," the sachem replied. "We have had traitors in the past."

"Do you suspect anyone?" said the old sanop as he reached for his ax. "If you do I'll slay him before he can do harm."

"Put away your tomahawk! Sassacus, alone, has power to strike down any traitor. I'll watch until I have proof. Remember Wequash. Because he turned to the English, his own clan has rejected him. If we had struck, they would have turned against their own nation."

As the old brave settled back on his mat, John saw that the two girls had come in. They stared as if they were trying to understand what was going on. He could see that they were frightened by the violence of the old sanop.

I wonder if they are going to ask me to question them? John thought. Then Kithansh came into the lodge.

John remembered how proud Kithansh was of his few

English words. The young sachem started to talk to the girls. John could see that they were becoming more and more frightened as he tried to make them understand by shouting and sign language. When he seized one of the muskets and thrust it at them, the girls cringed behind Wegun.

Kithansh turned to Mononotto and said, "The young squaws fear me because I am a warrior. If one of their own age, who is not a taker of scalps, spoke to them they would not hide behind Wegun as they do. Let Cheegut speak for us."

"It is not well for a wonnux to speak for the Pequotoog," the old sanop said. "How are we to know that he will give true answers. Ask Mommenoteck to come."

"Cheegut does not speak with a double tongue!" Mononotto said. "We'll do as Kithansh says. Why should we trouble Mommenoteck. You do not believe what he says when he tells you of the English." Turning to John, he said, "Ask the older one if she has knowledge of the white man's weapons."

John turned to Susan and said, "Do not be afraid. Kithansh is not going to hurt you. He is excited because you do not understand his English, of which he is very proud. He wants to know if you have knowledge of muskets and powder."

Then he added, "Go near to the young man and look in his face when you speak. Show him you are no longer afraid of him and that you understand what he is trying to say. Don't look my way. I'll translate for you."

Susan came from her refuge behind Wegun and walked slowly to Kithansh. She looked up at him and managed to give him a weak smile. The young sachem's face relaxed.

"I have never shot a musket," she said as she shook her head and pointed to the row of weapons on the mats. She touched one with "A.S." carved on the stock. "This is my father's. He said I was too young to shoot it. He was going to teach me next year." Her eyes filled with tears.

John translated to Kithansh, in a low voice, as Susan spoke.

"Cheegut has calmed the young squaw's fears of me," the young noble said, turning to Mononotto. "See how she smiles and tells me all. She says she is not old enough to learn the ways of the bushkeagun. That is her father's, which you see marked in that manner."

"Can you make the black sand?" Kithansh asked.

John translated and Susan said, "Only a few men know how. There are several things they grind together in a wooden mortar with a wooden pestle. I do not know what these things are, but I think one of them is charcoal."

"It is magic," said a sanop. "Their powows make this strong medicine. Capture one of them and make him tell the secret."

While they were talking, a messenger arrived. He seemed excited and angry. "The wonnux have captured four of our sanops," he said to Mononotto. "They send a message by the Dutch: 'Give us back our children, unharmed, and we return your braves. Torture them and we do the same to your four warriors.'"

"We can get nothing more from these young ones," Mononotto said. "Let us return them to the English and take their ransom."

"The wonnux say, 'We hold that which is of more value

140

than trade goods and wampum. That price we pay and nothing more.' "

Mononotto was silent for a moment. Then he said, "Take the payment. Send the girls to the Dutch. Tell them to give the children to the English when our sanops are freed."

"It shall be done," the messenger said. "The Dutch wait in the Pequots' river with their great canoe."

Mononotto turned to John and put his hand on his shoulder. "Tell the young squaws that we wish them no harm," he said. "Ask them to remember that Wegun has been good to them and that all the Pequotoog are not evil. Say then that they are free to go to the English."

Both girls started to cry when John told them they were free. They turned to Wegun and Susan said, "We'll never forget what you have done for us—you and your husband. Someday we may be able to repay you."

When John translated, Wegun said, "I have done as any woman should. Ask them to tell the English to be kind to captive Indian women and children." She turned to John. "What can these children do to help soften the blows our people will suffer?" She shook her head. "But I'm glad they are now happy."

Wegun found clothes that fitted the girls. She spent some time going from lodge to lodge to pick up dresses the raiders had brought back.

As the girls were ready to leave, Susan said, "Shall we tell them to rescue you, too? They don't know you are a captive. We can tell them all about your being taken prisoner and that you're not a runaway."

"No," John said after a moment's hesitation. "I'll stand

141

by Wegun and her family."

He walked with them to the brow of the hill, where they could see the masts of the squat Dutch vessel. Then he said, "Good-by, Susan and Hepsy. I don't think I'll ever see you again."

The next two days were anxious ones. Each time a messenger came to Weinshauks the squaws gathered to gossip. Then they returned to their lodges to sit in misery until their sanops returned to demand food.

Wegun heard only the news that her servant brought her. She turned to John and said, "I hope the white girls are safe with their own people. Now it looks like a storm."

"Heavy clouds are gathering," said the old squaw as she brought in an armload of wood. "Little bit of rain now. Soon, a big lot."

"Why is everything so quiet in the village?" John asked.

"There is a meeting of the council. Mononotto has been called," Wegun said. "I think it means more raids on the settlements where the Pequotoog strike and move on to another place."

"The whites gather their forces at the mouth of the great river," she continued. "We have to keep our village well guarded because it is where they will strike. Now we wait and are afraid. Even the dogs are silent."

John could hear faint sounds from the great lodge. Occasionally a voice was raised and then quickly hushed. After a time he saw the councilors file out and hurry toward their lodges with blankets shielding them from the rain that now poured down.

Mononotto came in and sat before the fire to dry. He

stared into the flame on the low hearth. Wegun put her finger on her lips and motioned to John.

After a few minutes the sachem shrugged. "It has come," he said. "More and more whites come to their fort and there are great canoes anchored there waiting to bring them to battle. Now we'll have to meet them without the guns, as we have no powder to put in them." He tossed a stick into the fire. "See how it snaps! It will do no good to spit in the hearth, there are too many of them." He wrapped his blanket about him and went out into the rain.

"When the rain stops will they dance about Guldooke?" John asked.

"It will be just before battle. I have seen the war dance many times, and the Pequotoog have always been victors. Now we face magic powers and everyone is afraid. It is hard to go into battle without being able to hurt the enemy."

Before John went to bed, Wegun said, "Sit beside me, Cheegut, I have much to tell you."

She was silent for some time. Then she said, "You must know that this is the greatest trouble our nation has ever had. It is all leading to ruin. No one can stop it."

"I knew there was much fear," John said, "but I didn't think it was hopeless."

"Have you noticed, the young men and boys have not been with you as much as they were several moons ago?"

"I have, but I thought it was because of all the preparations for war."

"It is more than that. Some of the Pequots now think of you as an enemy. They say you will help the English when we go into battle. Some of them think the white girls will tell that you are here and that will bring more evil on us."

Wegun paused so long that John thought she had finished. As he made a move to get up, she put out her hand. "I have thought of something you can do to please me," she said.

"What I have to ask will be hard for both of us, but it will be better in the end. My people were the Narragansetts. They are friends of the English and will help both of us if they can. Tomorrow I want you to go, as you did once before, to my mother. Stay with her. When the trouble is over you can return to us."

John thought for a time. Then he turned to Wegun. "I'll go as you ask, but when you need me I'll come back—no matter what the others think of me."

"It is well, muckachuck. Prepare for tomorrow's journey. Go at dawn—and do not look back!"

John gathered his few possessions, ready to pack at dawn. He was sorry that he had to leave his bearskin. He put enough food in his pouch for the journey, and then lay down to sleep.

The next day he trotted over the familiar trail to the Narragansett village. Wegun's mother received him as if he were her own grandson. She prepared a bed for him. As she was putting mats and blankets on the springy branches, she said, "Someday we'll get your bearskin from the Pequotoog. You don't need it now, but it will be good for the winter. You were a brave muckachuck.

"Now I'll fix your hair and change the decoration on your moccasins and cape so you will look like our boys.

Your knife sheath is Narragansett. I can see Wegun's work on it." As she made the changes, she corrected his pronunciation of words that marked him as Pequot. "It is not well to speak in their dialect. We know that you are English, but to speak like a Pequot might set some of the boys against you."

During the next few weeks John made friends with the Narragansett boys. They hunted and fished together. He learned a game in which they kicked a ball and tried to get it over the opponent's goal. Many times he went with them to the landing place, several miles from the fort.

One day the grandmother called John and said, "Does the name Kiswis mean anything to you?"

"Yes," he replied. "It is the name of a sanop who made trouble for me whenever he could."

"Then you'll not be sad at the news I give you. For several moons Kiswis has been living with the English at the fort they call Saybrook. He has eaten their meat and done squaw's work for them."

"He was mean, but I didn't think he would be a traitor to his own people," John said.

"He was not a traitor. He is now quite a hero. He lived with the English to find out what they were going to do. He had learned their language but pretended he did not understand the white men. When they sent their braves to the north, he would warn the Pequotoog and they would raid to the east.

"The English knew that someone was telling this. They thought that Uncas, the Mohegan, spoke with a double tongue. To show that he was loyal to the whites, Uncas killed three Pequots and captured Kiswis. He brought the heads and his prisoner to the fort.

"They tied Kiswis to a stake, just outside the walls, and started the torture. Uncas called to the English sachem, named Mason, as he waved the fresh scalps, 'See. Uncas and the Mohegans fight for the English. We killed the Pequotoog and this is how we treat the spy who told your secrets.'

"Another white sachem, called Underhill, shouted, 'It is not the custom of the English to torture our captives, even if they are spies.' He raised his bushkeag and killed Kiswis before he could suffer any more.

"The Mohegans were angry at losing their sport. They took his scalp, and would have eaten his flesh—as is the custom of the 'Man-eaters'—had not the English taken his body to bury it in their fashion."

"I'm sorry that Kiswis had to die in that manner," John said. "He was always my enemy, and did much harm to me. But I never wanted anything like this to happen to him."

"The Great Spirit takes care of his children in his own way," the old woman said. "We must accept what he sends."

John awoke the next morning to hear the wind roaring about the walls of the lodge. He looked from the doorway to see bits of thatch and bark, torn from the lodges across the dancing place, whirl by. Whirlpools of dust marched over the open space, picking up twigs and grass as they went.

A group of boys went by. "Come to the landing place," one of them shouted. "There are five great winged canoes. Their wings are folded and they toss in the angry waters."

John grabbed a handful of dried corn and rushed out to join them. The wind came from the southeast. It was warm and very strong. The boys braced themselves as they beat their way to the hill, overlooking the landing place.

The waters of the Narragansetts' bay were whipped into foam. As far as John could see, the whitecaps rushed toward the beach and broke in a steady roar. The vessels were anchored out beyond the line of surf, with their sails tightly furled. Masts whipped back and forth as the vessels tossed and spray dashed high over the hulls.

"I can see some red men in the great canoes," John said. "How did they get out there in this heavy sea?"

"They are not from our nation," one boy said. "They are Mohegans. Some of them live near the Pequot country and others come from the great river valley to the west. They are fierce warriors."

"I'm glad they are on our side when we fight the Pequotoog," said another boy. "Can you see Uncas?"

"I can't see any of them from here to know them," said another. "The white people do not have their shining coats. They must save them for battle.

"They are so few that the mighty Pequotoog will make short work of them in spite of their magic. Our people promised to help them. I hope we don't have to fight the Destroyers."

For two days the wind blew without a pause. Then, suddenly, it was still and the morning dawned warm and sunny.

It was early in the day when John heard the sound of drums beating out a lively marching rhythm. He rushed out and joined the crowd headed for the gateway. There

147

he saw a column of white men swinging along toward them in military formation. Their helmets and corselets gleamed in the sun. Flashes of light came from their muskets and the pikes or halberds that some of them carried.

John felt a rush of pride as he saw this group march so proudly. He counted seventy-seven white men in the group, and thought of the thousand warriors that Sassacus could put into battle. Following them was a small party of Mohegans, looking fierce in their war paint. They stared straight ahead as if they were not aware of the Narragansetts who watched them.

The white leader was a big man with a broad, bearded face. He moved lightly, in spite of his size. When the column reached a point just outside the gate, he called out a command in a loud voice. The tiny army halted. Then, at another command, the soldiers lowered their weapons to rest on the ground.

"Captain Underhill!" said the leader. "Take command. I will see Canonicus and request permission to pass through the Narragansett country."

"Yes, Captain Mason," Underhill replied as he swaggered forward. He signaled to the men and their Mohegan allies to stand at ease. Then he looked about him, with quick glances, and put his hand to his sword hilt so that the blade swung out straight behind him.

Captain Mason strode through the opening, dwarfing the Narragansetts who stood guard. John and the village boys followed the bearded warrior as he walked along with his great sword swinging at his side. "He is one of the 'long knives,'" said one of the boys. "They are great fighters."

They fell back when Canonicus approached, but not too far. The king greeted the commander, and one of the white men interpreted.

"This is a dangerous thing that you do, with so few warriors," Canonicus said. "The Pequotoog are fierce and Sassacus is crafty. We thought, when we made the treaty with the English, that you had more warriors than this."

"We do not need more. We have armor and muskets," Mason said. "Our Great Spirit fights with us because we all believe in Him. His help is more than the might of our long knives and guns."

"He must be great to give you so much courage," the king replied. "The warriors that my nephew, Miantonomo, will take, when he goes with you, will protect you. They will watch to see how brave the white men are when they hear the war cry. The Destroyers know no fear."

"All that we ask is permission to cross your country and to have guides to show the way. This is according to the treaty. We have a map, given us by your white father, which shows part of the way, but it is not enough. It does not show secret trails and places where we might be ambushed."

"Permission is granted. Miantonomo will go with you to see that no one breaks the promises of the talking leaves. His warriors will march on all sides. Five hundred sanops will protect you.

"Your guide is a former Pequot noble, named Wequash. He hates his former people and will lead you to their forts. Their places of ambush are known to him and he will warn you."

"Can we trust this man? Other Pequots have said they

were friendly and we have found them to be spies."

"Do you trust Uncas?" the king replied. "He was a Pequot, yet now he leads a band of fighting Mohegans. Wequash has been treated unfairly by his countrymen. Now he has accepted gifts from the English at Shawmut and will guide you where you want to go—even to death."

"When do we start?" Mason asked.

"Our braves assemble tonight. They will dance to prepare for the warpath. At dawn they march with you to the Niantic fort at Ninigret, where Sachem Wepitamock will give you food and shelter for the night. The next morning his braves will join you and our Narragansetts and go into the Pequot territory.

"But now is the time for your braves to rest, white captain. Come into the fort. We have prepared guest lodges for them. The squaws will cook food and prepare their beds."

The men stacked their guns and pikes outside the lodges. Then they removed their helmets and corselets. John saw that many had padded jackets instead of the breastplates and metal backs of the body armor. He fingered one of the jackets and found it was quilted and thick. "That should turn an arrow," he thought.

The owner of the jacket looked at him with a grin. "Look at him, Miles," he said to a companion. "These Injun youngsters are just as nosy as ours at home. Always meddling with things. Watch this." He picked up a musket and thrust it toward John. "Here. Want to take my gun?"

John drew back and put his hands behind him. The

soldiers laughed. "They think they're magic," one of them said.

If I can keep on fooling them, maybe I can slip away and join them as if I were really an "Injun." If Wegun ever needed help it will be now.

That night there was great excitement in the village. Streams of Indians poured into the open space, dogs barked and small boys dashed between the legs of the sanops. A huge fire blazed in the center of the dancing place. It shone on the faces of the ring of spectators and glinted on the armor of the English soldiers. Canonicus and Miantonomo sat cross-legged on a pile of mats. Near them, Captains Mason and Underhill, then Uncas with his Mohegans.

Across the circle were the drummers, gripping the short, hollow logs which were covered with tight skins. They watched Miantonomo for a signal, their hands poised to slap the drumheads. There were several in the group who held in their fists rattles made of tortoise shells filled with pebbles.

The young king nodded and the drummers started a slow, rhythmic beat that seemed to make the whole area throb. John waited with his Narragansett friends to see his first war dance.

Through a gap in the circle came a single file of Narragansett warriors. They were led by one of the younger sachems and they kept time with him in the slow, prancing steps. The line seemed endless as it swayed about the fire and completed a circle.

The sanops were dressed in loincloths and moccasins. Their bronzed bodies were oiled so that they gleamed in the firelight. The bunched feathers in their crests bobbed with them as they stepped along. Stripes of red and white paint were drawn across their bodies and faces. Dark eyes gleamed through these savage masks.

The throb of the drums and the swish of rattles quickened. The dance steps were more violent. Warriors leaped into the air and struck out with their tomahawks and war clubs.

A savage chant was started and became louder as they danced faster. Each warrior sang of combat, death to foes, scalps, great honor. John could not understand what they sang, but was able to pick out a few of the words. At intervals they gave loud cries and leaped high in the air as they swung their weapons. John felt as if he were under a spell. He could feel himself swaying with the sound and almost leaping as the braves gave their war cry.

The drums roared with a quick beat, and then all was still. The dancers stopped and faced the two kings. Miantonomo rose and spoke in a loud voice.

"Narragansett braves will show the white people how to face a deadly foe," he shouted. "When the wonnux blood turns to water, the Narragansetts will protect them. There will be great honor to all who bring back Pequot scalps. The whites and the Mohegans will learn how to fight, by watching you."

The moment he finished, the drums roared and the ring of warriors fought a battle in pantomime; whirling, striking, and shouting their defiance. The drums and rattles dropped into a slow, syncopated beat, with drums, then rattles alternating. The warriors danced out with a hop on each foot in time to the beat. The space was suddenly empty, as when water is poured from a jug. Color and sound seemed washed out of the scene. John thought that even the fire now seemed lifeless. He could hear a sound, like a deep sigh, from the spectators.

Canonicus rose, and all was silence. "See, O white men. The might of my nation stands with you in your fight against the enemy Pequotoog. The Destroyers are fierce and mighty, but Miantonomo, with his five hundred sanops, will save you when you run from the foe."

Captain Mason arose. John realized how big he was when he compared him with nearby Indians. He spoke in a firm voice, and an interpreter repeated his words in the Narragansett tongue. "Know, O King, that English soldiers do not run from their enemies! We ask that your braves stand by, as you promised in the treaty, and do not turn against us."

"It is well, Captain Mason," Canonicus said. "What the Narragansetts say—that they will do. You have seen our young braves in the dance. They are but a small part of our army. They will be well led. My nephew will go with them and fight by your side."

The fire was now a pile of red embers. A cool breeze blew gently across the dancing ground as Indians and Englishmen went to their lodges.

John was now sure that he would be able to join this force in the morning. His body relaxed and he slept.

Chapter Eleven

THE ENGLISH STRIKE

✝ JOHN awoke at the first sign of dawn. The night before seemed like a dream, a nightmare of naked, savage forms leaping to the deadly throb of the drums. *I'll join them, as if I belonged,* he thought. *I'll take my pack and keep out of the way of anybody who knows me.*

After a hasty meal he hurried out to join a group of Narragansetts. Several of the younger braves laughed at him but did nothing to drive him away.

All that John owned he carried in his pouch and blanket pack. He wore his knife and carried the war bow with its quiver of arrows slung over one shoulder. It was easy to mix with the braves and not attract too much attention.

Miantonomo sent out an advance party of forty or fifty sanops. Several of the English soldiers went with them. In a few minutes the main body formed and filed out along the trail. The rear guard was made up of Uncas, with his Mohegans, and a few white men.

The day was warm. The trail to Ninigret was broad and well beaten. John was impatient to go faster, and then realized that six hundred men do not move with as much speed as one boy.

Late that afternoon they arrived at the Niantics' fort. It was located on a neck of land that stretched out into a

154

large pond. The ground was high and the palisaded fort could be defended by a few warriors stationed at the narrow passage. Across the pond, John could see a slim stretch of beach that separated the still water from the deep green of the sound. It was low land with dunes. Beach grass and low-growing shrubs showed green and gray against the great waters beyond.

"The Niantic sachem, Wepitamock, is afraid to let so many into his strong place," a young sanop said. "He fears the Pequotoog and doesn't want them to know he is giving too much help to their enemies. Those are two reasons why we are staying outside."

"We'll have to watch him and his tribe," said another brave. "They may send a message to Sassacus, hoping to win his friendship. That would mean ambush. We must not let even a field mouse get by tonight."

"Why did the English come this long way from their fort at Saybrook?" John asked. "They must have passed the two Pequotoog forts several days ago."

"That was wise of the white sachem," a sanop said. "When the Pequots saw his winged canoes, they were ready to fight the wonnux as they came ashore. The whites would be wading, a few at a time, and a thousand Pequots would have smothered them. Now they think the English are afraid, because they sailed past. They shouted insults at them, hoping they would turn and fight on the red men's conditions. Now *he* is the one to pick the time and place of battle. The white Mason is a wise sachem."

"He will come in behind them, before they know he is near," said another sanop. "He will now have five hundred brave Narragansetts with him."

"We will show the wonnux how to fight," shouted another brave.

"They are all boasters," growled a battle-scarred Mohegan who sat nearby. "Let them save their brave words until they hear the Pequot war whoop and see them come on to fight until they kill or are killed."

Miantonomo and Mason came from the fort and joined their groups. Soon John could see Indians and whites taking positions across the neck of land. He unrolled his pack and settled down near one of the Narragansett sanops.

"The sentries are close together," he said to the brave. "They can almost touch each other with arms outstretched."

"That's right," said the red man. "We keep close watch and there are others who sleep near each sentry, ready to take his place. If some Niantic should wish to go around by water, we have braves watching and listening. They are in a jug."

Before John went to sleep, one of the braves crept near to him and whispered, "We are watching you, boy. We do not know if you are white boy, Pequot, or Narragansett. We take no chances on your getting away to warn Mononotto. Now sleep, and be sure you *do* sleep. No harm will come to you if you stay with us. I'll be watching."

John awoke when a gentle hand touched his shoulder. "Wake up, young one," said his companion of the night before. "The sun will soon rise. Wash yourself. It will be a hot day."

All about him there was a stir as white men and Indians lashed their packs and ate dried food. One Narragansett was boasting loudly to several Englishmen.

"I don't know what the Injun is talking about," one of the soldiers said, "but it sounds insulting."

"Don't pay him any heed," said his companion. "They talk big now, but just wait!"

The English soldiers kneeled and their chaplain prayed aloud for strength and guidance. John tried to remember some of the prayers his mother had taught him. The Indians stood by in silence as they watched this strange thing.

As the army moved toward the Pequot border, the sun rose higher and beat down hotter. "This is awful hot!" said one English soldier during one of the halts. "I never felt it so hot in May. Wish I could get rid of this padded jacket."

"If you want to feel hot, just wear one of these corselets. You'll freeze in winter and roast in summer."

The army halted at the ford in the Pawcatuck River. John took off his clothes and plunged into the water. He soaked in it as long as he dared, and then dressed, ready to go on.

"From now on be especially alert," Captain Mason ordered. "We enter the Pequot territory when we get to the other side of the Pawcatuck. Wear your body armor and your helmet no matter what it costs you in comfort. Inspect your muskets. Blow out the pans and put in fresh priming powder. One man in each file will keep a match burning to fire the guns."

"The Narragansetts are deserting in droves," Underhill said as he walked over to his commander. "Several hundred of them dropped to the rear. I just got word they are now on their way back to their fort."

"I'm not worried. Remember how the Great Jehovah

commanded that Gideon reduce his army. They fought and defeated the Midianites with but few men, and the help of the Almighty. We have everything that Gideon had."

John's Indian companion of the previous day was missing, as well as many others he knew by sight. Now there were about a hundred of them left. These looked about them anxiously.

One of the Mohegans said, "They talk big. Now they run away. Our forty Mohegans are worth their whole army because we are not afraid. Pequots are only men, and men can die."

"You speak well," said Captain Mason. He turned to Underhill. "It was well that we weeded out those Englishmen who were not strong in body and in spirit. They will serve to guard the fort."

The afternoon was torture for most of the whites. John could see some of them staggering along without packs, while others carried a double load. Evening brought a little relief from the heat. They caught glimpses of the Pequot harbor as Wequash led them along back trails.

John overheard the guide tell Mason, "All day the Pequots feast and dance. They have done this for three days or more, since you passed by in your ships. Sassacus has sent three hundred sanops from Weinshauks to go on big raids. Seven hundred Pequots are in Mystic fort now. That is why they have war dance. Hear their war whoops?"

John could hear the sound of drums and savage yells.

Soon they came to a crossing that John remembered. It was at the head of the cove. Wequash pointed out a place that John had never seen before. It was a sheltered area almost surrounded by rocky banks. They entered through the narrow opening.

"We are now about two miles from the Pequot fort," Mason said to his men. "Take care that you make no noise or show any lights. Conceal the glow of your matches. Each man is to be sure his musket is primed and that he has a good length of match.

"Now eat your food uncooked. Get as must rest as you can, because we attack before dawn."

"You watch for shkook." Wequash advised. "Him plenty bad."

The soldiers hunted out several rattlesnakes, which they killed. Then they made their preparations for the night. A few of them on sentry duty stayed near the entrance with some of the Mohegans.

"They make plenty noise," said one Mohegan to his companion. "Soon they will be much tired and sleep until we wake them with a tomahawk."

"Seven hundred will be heavy work to wake up that way," the Mohegan replied. "We have big fight ahead of us."

A bright full moon was rising. It shone into the rocky entrance, casting black shadows. Mist rose from the harbor. A wind from the northeast blew the chilly moisture into their camp. John pulled his blanket about him *I'll get away, during the fight, and go to Weinshauks*, he thought. Then he went to sleep.

John awakened from a sound sleep. He became aware of a stir about him. He opened his eyes and looked in dismay. It was bright, too late for the attack. Then he realized it was the full moon in a cloudless sky. He made his pack, ate a handful of food, and was prepared for any opportunity that might let him escape to Weinshauks.

There were Indians on all sides of him, some of them watching. The white men were too busy to notice an "Indian" boy.

The two captains inspected their soldiers to see that muskets were primed and loaded. Soldiers helped each other fasten buckles on their armor or adjust pack straps.

Captain Mason said, "Mr. Stone, will you lead in prayer?"

All of the white men knelt with their helmets between their knees, while the chaplain asked the aid of the Almighty. The Indian allies looked on in astonishment. Some of them got on their knees as they saw the white men do, hoping to share in their magic.

As they moved out of the enclosure, the chill of the morning mist and the excitement and fear of the coming attack made John shiver. He clenched his jaws to keep his teeth from chattering.

Mason and Underhill walked ahead with Wequash. The soldiers and Mohegans followed in single file, along the narrow trail. They had gone about two miles when they stopped. John saw Mason and Wequash whispering. Then the Indian pointed up the steep hill and John saw that they were close to the palisades. *How different this is from the first time I saw the fort,* John thought. *Then there was noise and excitement. I thought I was going to be killed. Now they're all asleep.*

There was a short conference, and Underhill signaled his men and moved off toward the south. Mason waited a few minutes and motioned his men to advance from the northeast. Matches gleamed as his men deployed and made ready to fire a volley from their matchlocks.

"You dare not attack these fierce Pequots," Miantonomo whispered as he and a few Narragansetts huddled near Mason. "Go away now, while there is yet time. Save yourselves."

Captain Mason looked at the sachem with contempt. "Go to a safe distance with your brave warriors," he said. "Watch and see how an Englishman fights." He moved forward, sword in hand.

All was silent in the fort. Then a dog barked, and another. A voice screamed, "Wonnux! The wonnux have come!"

There was a volley from the muskets of Mason's men. A moment later came the roar of guns from Underhill's attacking party. The soldiers reloaded and primed their weapons and moved toward the gateway. Some of them struggled to get through the stiff branches. Mason cut his way through the barrier, swinging his sword like a sickle. The soldiers fired another volley and Mason entered the fort followed by his men. The Pequots fired a shower of arrows, which glanced off their helmets and body armor. John could hear yells of dismay from the red men.

As the last Englishman entered the fort, a number of the Indians ran toward the woods. John saw his chance and crawled around the palisade to a trail that he remembered. He crouched as he moved along out of possible sight of the attacking party. Then he rose and ran until he reached the next hill.

He stopped to look back. He heard shouts of the white men and occasional musket shots. The war whoops of the

161

Pequots became fewer and now he could hear the wild yells of the Narragansetts and Mohegans. There was a thin stream of smoke that grew thicker as he watched. It blew toward the south and then, suddenly, it broke into flame. Soon the whole village was blazing and he could hear the screams of Indians caught in the conflagration.

From his position on the hill he could see figures climbing to the tops of the palisades and jumping to the ground outside. Some fell back into the flames that were filling the whole enclosure. Those who reached the clearing outside of the fort ran toward the woods. In the light of the rising sun, John could see bands of Indians clubbing and scalping the escaping Pequots.

"Some of them were my friends," John said to himself. "No matter what crimes any of them have committed, this is a horrible way to pay for it. Will Weinshauks be next?"

When he reached the village, he found the whole place aroused. Warriors were at the gate, waiting for their leaders to appear. Then Sassacus and Mononotto arrived and led several hundred sanops out of the gateway, on the run. Their weapons were ready and their faces set in scowls of anger and hate.

John hurried to Wegun's lodge and found her with her arms around Nemud. "Why have you come back, Cheegut?" she said. "You were safe with my people. How can we protect you from the Pequotoog? You are English and it is the English who have attacked."

"I have come back to be with you and Nemud," John replied. "You are all I have and I'm going to stay and help."

"You are a good muckachuck," Wegun said, "but I fear for you. Tell me! What have you seen?"

John related all that had happened from the time he had gone to join her mother at Narragansett. She shuddered as he described the last view he had of the burning fort.

"Now I know that our sanops will be too late to help," Wegun said. "It must have been hard for you to see the Pequotoog and the bearded long-knives fight each other. You are fond of one and cannot side with them because you are white."

Chapter Twelve
DEATH OF A NATION

THE sun was high when the sanops returned to Weinshauks. There was a burst of loud talk when Sassacus strode in. His face was without expression as the Pequotoog crowded about him. They shook their fists and shouted that he was to blame for all that had happened.

One noble approached the silent king and extended his knife toward him, hilt first. "You have caused this tragedy with your desire for revenge!" he shouted. "Take this knife and slay all your family and yourself. Let no more, with the blood of your father, cause us trouble."

Sassacus looked at him, snorted, and then turned away.

"We are all Pequotoog," Mononotto said as he pushed between the angry sanop and the king. "The answer is not to shed more blood but to save what is left of our nation."

"Seven hundred of our warriors have died or been enslaved in one span of the sun's journey," the sanop snarled. He thrust the knife toward Sassacus once more. "Some were killed by the guns and the long knives, but most perished by the fire. Those who escaped the fort were slain or captured by the Mohegans and Narragansetts, who leaped out like wolves from their hiding places. Our sanops were too tired and burned to fight. It was you who sent hundreds there from Weinshauks to die with them. Kill yourself and join them if you wish to keep your honor!"

"The king has been wise in many things," Mononotto said as he struck the knife to the ground. "Did not a council of nobles decide to send the reinforcement to the Mystic fort to make ready for war against the wonnux? Was it the king's fault that they were surprised by a crafty foe? Those who died were to blame for thinking the white people had passed by in fear. Where were their outposts? Who made them tired with feasting and dancing all the day before and far into the night?"

"Mononotto speaks truly," said another noble. "Now that we know the white people are brave and have crafty leaders we shall take no more chances. Let us prepare to defend this fort with all our remaining strength."

"Do we need to defend it now?" said a sanop. "We chased the wonnux to the river, where they sailed away in haste. We saw them go toward their fort at Saybrook. We have frightened them!"

"You make the same mistake that was made by those who died," Mononotto said. "They will return with more warriors to destroy what is left of the Pequotoog. Our safety lies in fighting as red men. Seek the woods and swamps where our woodcraft and quickness of movement protect us. Forts can be blazing traps."

Sassacus, who had been silent until this moment, said, "Prepare to leave Weinshauks, as Mononotto says. Take what can be carried with us and burn what is left. Go now while there is yet time."

There were murmurs of agreement as the group broke up.

John could hear the wailing of squaws for their lost sanops and for the suffering to come. Children cried because they were confused. Even the village dogs slunk behind the lodges and lay with their jaws on the ground. They did not have enough spirit to hunt for fleas.

"Here is a white boy," one sanop cried as he grabbed John. "Let us kill him as we shall slay all our captive whites!"

"Let him go!" said Mononotto as he released the boy and pushed the sanop aside. "The muckachuck is mine. He saved my son. When he could have gone with the English he returned to us. Do not dare threaten him again! He is my son."

Squaws piled dry brush against the lodge walls, ready for the torch. Others uncovered their scanty stores of dried food and stowed them in carrying baskets.

Scouts came into the fort throughout the next few days, bringing news of the English soldiers' movements at Saybrook and along the coast.

"Do not go far from Weinshauks," Mononotto said. "The enemy red men are all about. Several of our sanops have been killed and scalped."

"When the wonnux come, we'll hide at Ohomowauke," one sanop said. "There at the Owl's Nest the squaws and children will be safe while we fight."

"That is not wise," Mononotto said. "The place is known to all our red-men enemies. They know that we go there when the winters are too cold to stay here on the hill. It will be a trap. Our safety is in the wooded country north of the Mohegans, along the great river. When we are again strong, we'll return."

"We're not going to run like frightened rabbits," the sanop replied. "I'll go to Owl's Nest with my clan. A hundred of us will be safe. You can go your own way."

Mononotto shook his head and walked away.

Late in June a scout reported, "The English are getting ready. Wonnux come from the river villages, others from Shawmut, and some from the colony in the land of Massasoit."

Each day scouts reported more white men, more ships at the mouth of the Connecticut River. War parties of Mohegans and Narragansetts, made bold by the destruction at Mystic, raided the camps of squaws and sold the women as slaves. Hunting parties were no longer safe. Small groups were killed or captured to be tortured.

"When we leave Weinshauks now, we'll have to go in full force." Sassacus said. "No small parties are to go from the protection of the walls."

One day a sanop dashed into the fort. He was bleeding from a hatchet wound and was so tired he could hardly stand. "Where is Sassacus?" he said. "I have a message for him."

"Speak. It is Sassacus," said the king, who had hurried from his lodge.

"The wonnux are on the warpath once more! There are many winged canoes, filled with white warriors, coming toward our shores. The hostile red men are gathering so that we cannot fight off the whites and our enemies on the beach. We must go to the woods and leave the great water."

When all was ready, Sassacus gave the word and the band of about six hundred Indians—braves, women, and children—filed out of Weinshauks. They stood, silently, at the foot of the hill while sanops thrust torches into the piles of brush. As the flames roared high, John could hear the sound of weeping.

One party headed for Owl's Nest, and the main party moved toward the setting sun.

"Keep as near the shore as possible," said Mononotto. "We must get food from the sound. And you, Cheegut, guard the women and children from any who might slip by our sanops."

When other Indians came in to relieve the boys, they went to the shore to search for clams or fish. English sailing vessels patrolled constantly, so they could not dig clams or spear fish. They looked for telltale holes that marked the beds of the long-necked clams, and returned to dig in darkness. Sometimes they got enough to fill their net bags. Again they would return with nothing.

The braves were forced to keep together in strong parties. Hostile Indians darted in to attack or attempted ambush along their route. Night after night there would be weeping of squaws who had lost a brave that day.

One day as they were scouting along the shore, they came to a point of land jutting out into the sound. Duksors pointed to a tree that stood near the water. "Look!" he said. "The head of Mausaumpous. He was one of Sassacus' brothers."

John saw the sachem's head wedged into the crotch and facing the broad water.

"I hope they didn't have time to torture him," John said.

Each day there were fewer in their party. Squaws and children sickened and died, to be buried where they last camped. John could hear the triumphant whoops of the enemy coming closer each day.

One evening Sassacus called the remaining nobles together. "We must go into hiding," he said. "There is a swamp, in the land of the Paugasucks, that will not trap us as Owl's Nest has trapped the Beaver Clan. Some were slain. The others were sold as slaves to work in the hot islands to the south."

"What of the plan to reach the highlands of the great river?" Mononotto asked.

"That plan is still good," replied the king. "I go, with twenty sanops, to find the way and to parley with the Mohawks for protection. In their country we'll be safe. No man, red or white, dares go against this terrible nation on the great river.

"Go with the remaining sanops and the others who are left," Sassacus continued. "Ask the Paugasucks for shelter. If they do not give it willingly—take it. Stay in their village as long as you can. If the enemy should come, hide in the swamp called Unkuowa, where you cannot be found. When I have made the treaty, I'll return. The Mohawks will send warriors to guard us on our way to their land."

Without any further words the king slipped away, followed by his party. They headed north toward the land of the Mohawks.

Mononotto and his group dragged themselves westward. They were weak with hunger. Each day the sanops were able to move shorter distances away from the main body. Their numbers were diminishing and they had to close their ranks. When they came to the Housatonic River, the braves fanned out to the rear and along the bank. John could hear the shouts of the Mohegans as they closed in. One loud-voiced Indian shouted, "Now we'll get you, Pequotoog! You won't get away!"

Mononotto said to John, "I have need of your help. I am going to swim across to talk to the Paugasuck sachem. While I am gone, you must get the women and children across the river. The braves will be busy keeping back our enemies. I know you can do this because you are wise in the ways of the water."

"Do you remember how the sanops planned the other river crossings?" John said to Duksors and Bopoose. "Let us do the same. Work fast while our sanops hold back the Mohegans."

They gathered their friends to scout the shore for material. When they had enough logs and branches, they lashed them together with twisted vines to make two rafts.

"Each of you take charge of a raft," John said to the two boys. "Pick two or three who can swim to help you. I'll be ready to help if anything goes wrong.

"It is good the river is sluggish and the water low. In the spring it would have been different. Now work carefully and put those who cannot swim well in the center. Others can hang on and float across with you. Push out until you can no longer wade and then swim, pushing the raft, to that sandy cove over there. Unload quickly and push back for another trip."

John helped load and trim the rafts. He was constantly in and out of the water. In the distance he could hear frequent sounds of fighting. It seemed to be coming nearer. When they had ferried the last group across, they waded ashore and stretched out on the ground in the warm sun.

"Now I know why the Great Spirit sent you back to us," said Wegun. "You have ferried nearly two hundred people across the river and no one has been lost."

When John saw the first of the Pequotoog appear in the clearing across the river, he signaled to the boys to get the rafts to the other side. As they neared the other shore several of the sanops were swimming.

"Get our wounded, muckachucks," said one. "They cannot swim. We'll help you with the rafts."

Some of the wounded were able to walk. Others were carried to the rafts. Then, with the sound of battle close behind them, they pushed off for the friendly shore. They were hardly in midstream when the remaining sanops fired a shower of arrows at the Mohegans and then dashed for the river, to swim and dive away from the missiles that zipped into the water all around them.

"Good muckachucks!" shouted the sanops as they gathered around the boys and slapped them on their backs. They waited for a short time, resting and binding up the wounds of those who had been hurt. Across the water, the Mohegans shouted and waved their war clubs. "Brave Pequots!" they yelled. "You run away. Soon you cannot run any more."

Mononotto arrived and beckoned to the sanops. "We go to the village near Unkuowa. The Paugasucks are fearful. I told them to say to our enemies, 'The Pequotoog forced me.' They will give us food and shelter in their lodges, and guides to the great swamp, if we have to hide."

"Can we trust the Paugasucks?" asked a sanop.

"Can we trust our own?" Mononotto replied. "One of our sanops, Cushawaset, whom the wonnux call 'Luz' for some reason, has run away to join them. He must have felt that our cause was hopeless and so he has deserted. He heard Sassacus speak of the village and swamp. If he can find Unkuowa, he will lead the English there.

"Let us go to the village. We know of this treachery and can be on our guard. It will not be long before Sassacus returns with the Mohawks. Then we'll all be safe."

They reached the Paugasuck village just before dark. A few Indians shuffled out to meet them. Others peeped out from their huts or from the tangled undergrowth beyond the clearing. John looked about him at the sprawling village. It was dirty and it smelled of sewage and unwashed bodies.

The Paugasuck squaws crept in with baskets of food. They put them on the floor and scurried out. The Pequot women went to work, preparing a meal, as if they were back in Weinshauks.

"You bring us bad things," said one wrinkled Paugasuck squaw. "Mohegans and whites come soon. Kill us because we help you."

"You were forced to help us. They cannot punish you for that," said Wegun. "Someday when we are strong again you will be glad because we will be your friends."

The Pequot sanops came in, a few at a time, to gulp the hot food and return to their guard duty far out from the village.

"Do not fear," Tassaquanot said. "No one can get past us." But all of them *did* fear. They remembered Cushawaset.

It was nearly noon of the third day in the village when a Pequot scout ran in shouting, "The wonnux come!" He paused to catch his breath. "They move slowly and they are many. Mononotto says to go to the swamp. He will be there to show you the hidden paths and where to hide."

Wegun gathered the squaws to give them final instructions. There was a bustle in the guest huts and John could hear several children crying. Then they struggled along the road to the swamp, loaded with their blankets and provisions. The Paugasucks stood by without offering to help.

The swamp was a dismal place. Around the border John could see a tangled mass of joe-pye weed, goldenrod, tall fern, and spotted jewelweed. This was mixed with a network of cat brier with cruel thorns. Back of this he could see dense foliage of scattered willows, wild cherry, and alder. Brown swamp water oozed through the moss and rotted leaves as he stood there.

A small group of Paugasucks led them to an opening where a concealed causeway stretched across the swamp. Mononotto met them and said, "Follow me and watch where you step. Thick muck and deep holes hide under that surface of dead leaves and branches."

The view became clearer as they went deep into the swamp. John saw several places that he was sure would be safe. Tangled roots had built up small islands above the bog water. Groups selected these spots and went to work cutting branches to keep them clear of the dampness and to form screens for concealment. Clouds of mosquitoes gathered about them. "By and by more come. In night, plenty bad," one Paugasuck said. "Now we stay here. We afraid to go back. Wonnux kill."

The Pequots wrapped themselves in blankets and sweltered in the moist heat. Some of them gathered muck to plaster on the exposed parts of their bodies.

John could not count the Pequot sanops who slipped into Unkuowa. They seemed to come from several directions. When he saw no more activity, he was sure all were there who could come.

It was quiet for a time. Then John heard the crackling of brush and the sound of cutting and breaking of branches. There were confused sounds of struggle. An English voice called, "Help us! We're stuck in the mire and the thorns hold us fast!"

Then the sounds of struggle increased. Pequot yells were suddenly cut short. Then all was still.

After a time one of the sanops crawled across the causeway, and Wegun called to him. His arm was hanging by his side and blood dripped from a sword cut.

"Some of the wonnux rushed in," he gasped. "They got stuck fast in the thorns and sank deep in the muck. We wounded several of them, in spite of their armor. They cried for help and two others came to their rescue with their long knives. They killed the other Pequotoog and I am left with this wound. Heal me so that I can fight once more."

Wegun took spider web and puffball powder to make a pad and stop the bleeding. She tied this on with strips of bark and bound his arm to his side with hide thongs. "You cannot use that arm to fight. Rest and wait here for help to come. Sassacus will soon return with the Mohawks."

"We are surrounded," said a sanop who crawled past them. "The English are all about. We see them on all sides of the swamp."

There was a brief period of silence. Then a white man called from the edge of the swamp, speaking in the Pequot tongue, "I am called Thomas Stanton. I speak for this great army that surrounds you. There is no way for you to escape. Give up now so that no more lives will be lost."

"Sassacus will come with help from the Mohawks," called Mononotto. "He will be here soon. Be wise, white man, tell your army to run away while there is yet time. The Mohawks are greater warriors than any you have ever met."

"The Mohawks are friends of the English," Stanton replied. "We have nothing to fear from them."

"What makes you say they are your friends?" said Mononotto. "They promised to come to the aid of the Pequots if we were ever in trouble."

"This is what makes me say they are your enemies," Stanton said. Turning to one of the Mohegans, he continued, "Show the Pequots what you have. Do you know this person?"

Mononotto gasped, and a cry of horror went up from all who saw. "Where did you get the head of our king?" he asked.

"It was sent to us by the Mohawk sachem to whom Sassacus appealed," Stanton said. "The Mohawks slew all, and sent word that they were fighting on our side.

"Send out all who do not have English blood on their hands. We'll spare their lives. All others will be killed, according to the laws of our people."

John saw Mononotto's shoulders droop at the sight of the bloody head of Sassacus. Then the sachem raised his head and called, "We have innocent people with us who are not of the Pequotoog. We forced them to help us. These Paugasucks have done no harm. Will you spare them?"

"We'll spare them and any Pequot who is guiltless of killing white men."

"We are sending out the people of the village. The Pequotoog will never surrender. Here we fight to the end. If our nation dies, it will die here in Unkuowa. I have spoken, white man Stanton."

The unhappy Paugasucks crawled along the causeway, back to their huts in the dirty village. All about him John could see hopeless yet determined faces.

Soon they heard Stanton's voice from the edge of the swamp. "The Paugasucks are back in safety. Now change your minds, Pequotoog. Is it well for all to die because of a few? Give up the blood-guilty ones and come out in peace. Refuse, and we shoot into the swamp until all are dead."

"Take that for your insolence!" cried a sanop as he loosed an arrow. This was followed by a shower of missiles, several of which struck Stanton's corselet and helmet. He retired, hastily, with an arrow dangling from his sleeve.

"Lie down in the mire. Get behind any tree or mound that will give you shelter," Mononotto called. "Soon they will shoot the bushkeagun."

They cowered in the mud until after dark. There was a steady fire from the muskets. Snapping twigs reminded them that death was just a few inches above them. Some of the sanops died as they tried to get better bow shots at their attackers. The squaws dug shallow graves and covered the dead with mud. "We'll hide our weeping," one squaw said. "They must not know how many they have killed."

All during the night there were scattered musket shots. A few of the children slept in their mothers' arms, but everyone else was painfully awake, waiting for the dawn.

Birds made sleepy stirrings, and a faint glow showed from the east. Mononotto gathered his remaining sanops and said, "We must break through to the open country. Then we can attack the wonnux without being surrounded. If we are killed, our women and children will be spared. It is still dark. Let us go!"

John could hear no sound as the sanops wormed their way through the mire. He listened carefully. Then there were confused shouts from the Englishmen as the Pequots came out, fighting. There were some musket shots, then all was still. Off in the distance he heard a triumphant whoop and knew that some had broken through to the open.

As the sun rose, the survivors huddled in the muck, waiting for the end. John looked about him and could hardly recognize the creatures he saw. They had smeared mud on their skins to protect themselves from mosquitoes. It was caked in drying plates so they resembled some swamp animals.

Chapter Thirteen

END OF THE TRAIL

A LITTLE after sunrise the English crept into the swamp. John could hear them poking around in the mud and exclaiming each time they found a dead Indian. They dragged the bodies out to dry land and dug graves to bury them. Then they came back and herded the women and children before them.

"Stay with me," Wegun said as she drew Nemud and John close to her. "We'll face whatever comes to us. Now we must go with the English."

There were nearly two hundred squaws and children who formed the tattered dirty band that the soldiers herded to the shore. As they passed Cushawaset, the squaws spat at him and the older children called out, "Traitor!"

Three vessels were anchored offshore. Small boats were drawn up on the beach, and sailors stood ready to help load the prisoners aboard.

An officer divided the Pequotoog into three groups. He placed Wegun and her boys in the smallest. "Put these people in the pinnace," he said. "It'll hold about thirty, if you crowd them. They look as if they can stand an open boat better than most of them. Put the rest in the snow and the pink. They can be put below decks."

They huddled in the bottom of the open boat. Then sails were hoisted on both masts, and the light craft was on its way before the heavier vessels had started.

A young sailor scooped up a bucket of sea water and placed it in front of Wegun. She stared at it for a moment and then said, "To be clean is to get back some of our pride. Let us all wash."

Soon they were all busy getting rid of the caked mud and taking turns with the bucket. The sailor grinned and dipped up water for them until they were all partly clean.

The long night was chilly. A brisk wind blew spray into the open boat. The Indians huddled together and tried to protect themselves from the cold. Some of them slept.

In the early dawn they passed a large island with rolling hills. Wegun pointed toward it and said, "That must be Capawack. Some of the Wampanoags live there."

The sailor, seeing her point, said, "Martha's Vineyard. No white men live there." Then, seeing that she did not understand, he was silent.

There was food for them all, strange to their taste, but good to keep them alive. Many of them were sick from the lively motion of the pinnace and wanted nothing, but Wegun urged them to take some nourishment.

"Them Pequints is better off here in the open than the the ones under decks in the snow and the pink. It gets pretty foul below decks with only the crew. It must be bad with a load of smelly savages."

"These ones'll warm up soon enough after they are shipped to the Barbados to work in the fields," said another sailor.

"I'll wager you a shilling that the good-looking wench with the two boys will be grabbed for a house servant in the Bay Colony."

On the third day they sailed into Boston Harbor. John could not remember much of the city. He recognized the three hills and the stack of brushwood for a beacon, on top of one of them.

As they approached the wharf, he could see irregular streets lined with stout houses. They were neatly built of clapboard. Some were half timbered, with wattle and clay filling the spaces between the heavy beams. A few of the larger ones were made of brick. Thatch or shingles covered the roofs, and a few had diamond panes of window glass which glistened in the sun.

A small crowd waited on the shore. More people were coming. As the pinnace drew up to the dock and made fast, a dignified gentleman, dressed in dark clothes and fine white linen, came to meet them.

"Who's that?" said one of the Connecticut soldiers.

"That's Winthrop. He's the governor," a seaman answered.

"I've heard of him," the soldier continued. "They say he is a staunch Puritan, but kinder than most."

"Don't let the people of this colony hear you call them 'Puritans,'" said the seaman. "Some stout fellow will knock you down. Then he'll pray to be saved from damnation, because he had joy in doing it. The strict churchmen call themselves the 'People of God.' Remember that and save yourself a broken crown."

The captives crawled out on the dock. They were stiffened by three days in the boat and could hardly walk.

180

They hobbled past the governor, who stood watching with several of his companions.

"Why are there so few captives here?" the governor asked. "Are there no others?"

"Yes, Your Honor," replied the captain, touching his cap. "We have, in all, about ten score. A sorry lot they are. The others come in the slower vessels."

"We'll divide these as slaves for Connecticut and Massachusetts," the governor said. "I have a letter from Captain Stoughton, asking that he be given one of them, a strong squaw, for a house servant. He said he gave her a coat to cover her nakedness. She must be on one of the other vessels. There are several others who have done good service and should have slaves."

He turned to Wegun, who put her arms about Nemud and John. "This squaw looks intelligent," he said. "She will make a good house servant for some family. The boys can be sent to the West Indies to work in the fields."

John wanted to cry out about this, but determined to keep still and not be recognized as a white boy. He whispered to Wegun and told her what the governor had said.

Stanton, the interpreter, was standing nearby. He walked over to Winthrop and said, "Your Excellency, this is no common squaw. She is a royal princess of the house of Canonicus. She is wed to a Pequot sachem named Mononotto."

When Wegun heard the name Mononotto, she spoke hurriedly to Stanton.

"She has just asked," the interpreter said, "that she be not separated from her children and that her royal body be not degraded or insulted. Other than that she will meet whatever fate Your Excellency decides."

"I have heard that Mononotto is second to Sassacus. He took active part in the campaign against our people," the governor said. "Why should we show special consideration for his family?"

"It is well known," said Stanton, "that he has opposed Sassacus in many things. He wished to surrender the murderers. He wanted to remain friends with the white people. In all this he was overruled by the majority. He obeyed as a loyal Pequot, and served as an English soldier would who was under orders. Do you wish to punish that?"

While Stanton was talking, there was a slight commotion. John saw two girls pushing their way through the crowd to get a good look at the captives. He recognized the two as Susan and Hepsy Swain, the girls from the Wethersfield massacre.

"It is the good lady who saved us when we were about to be tortured," said Susan as she curtsied to the governor. "Do not harm her, sir. She is good and kind. Her name is Wegun, which means 'Good.' " She caught her breath and blushed.

"Tell me more," said Winthrop.

"The Pequots wanted to hurt us so we would tell them how to make powder and shoot muskets. She made them stop. The little boy is her real son. The big one is an English lad. He spoke both languages and helped her save us. Now he is adopted and his real name is John Bishop."

Winthrop turned to John and looked at him closely. "The boy is surely white!" he exclaimed. "Why have you been silent? Where did you come from?"

"I was bound to William Hoskins, at his farm near Wethersfield," John said. "I was treated like Wegun's son. Now I want to stay with her."

"I heard of this lad," one of the men said. "He was orphaned during that first winter of 1630 and bound to Hoskins for his board and keep. Hoskins moved to the Hartford Colony and took land there. We lost track of the family. Then we heard he was a runaway and that we were to be on the lookout for him."

"So you're a runaway!" the governor said. "Is that the reason you have kept silent?"

"I'm no runaway, sir!" John answered. "I was captured by the Pequots."

"When these girls were there, why didn't you let them tell us of your captivity?"

"Because I was happy with Wegun. It was my first real home since my mother died. If she is to be a slave, let me be with her."

"This woman will not be a slave," the governor said. "She has all the good qualities that many of our white people lack. Tell her that she and her family will be my guests until I can provide for each of you."

"Am I to return to the Hoskins family?" John asked.

"You cannot return to them. They were killed in one of the raids and their cabin burned.

"Send word to our soldiers and to the Narragansetts that Mononotto is to be spared," the governor said. "We'll examine his actions to see if he is as guiltless as Master Stanton says. If so we'll deal with him as an honorable foe."

John translated for Wegun. She held out her hands in

a gesture of thanks. Winthrop turned to a servant and said, "Take these people to my home. See that they are provided with baths and changes of clothes. They are to be my guests."

A motherly woman, the governor's housekeeper, said to John, "You're an English boy, aren't you? I heard tell that the Indians had stolen you away. Do you still speak English?"

"Yes. I have been with the Pequots only a bit over a year. I learned their language but haven't forgotten my own."

"Well, then, you just tell the Indian lady and the boy that we are heating water for baths. They can go out to the washhouse. Now just look at you! You've got dried dirt in your ears and hair. See to it that you scrub yourself."

"The soft stuff in the wooden bowls is called 'soap.' The English use it instead of sand. This rough cloth is a towel to dry yourself," John explained to Wegun. "There are clothes the white people wear on the bench. We'll take them with us when we go into the washhouse." John picked up his and felt of the stiff shoes.

"Have the white woman show me how to wear these," Wegun said. "It's not well to have the English laugh at me. I have the headband and belt in my pouch. They must not be destroyed. Everything else can be thrown away. They bring back bad memories."

When Wegun had gone into the washhouse, John spoke to the housekeeper who answered, "Bless her heart. I'll help her dress properly." She turned to John. "Was the life hard, being a captive of the Indians? Did they treat you well at all?"

184

"I was happy until this war started. Then we walked, and hid, and went hungry until the end."

She clapped her hands to her bosom. "You poor boys! I've been gabbing all this time and you never complained. Wait here and I'll bring you some buttered corn pone and milk."

It was John's first drink of milk since the loss of Daisy. The corn bread was golden brown and crisp. A thick spread of butter was slowly melting into the warmth.

"What is it, Cheegut? Is this wonnux food?" Nemud grabbed the trencher and the mug of milk. He sniffed at each.

"Taste and see. It may seem strange to you because of the salt, but it's like our corncake. The white stuff is called 'milk.' Drink it. It's good!"

Nemud sipped and made a face. He peeped over the rim of the mug and continued as he saw John doing. They both chewed on the corn bread. John saw a smile come over Nemud's face as he got the taste of the corn.

"The food is strange, but good," Nemud said. He licked the butter from his fingers and scraped up the crumbs from the trencher.

"The white person's moccasins are stiff and hard. The clothes are going to choke my body. I'll do as you do, but I don't know if I can stand these foolish things."

When Wegun appeared, John stared. The soft gray gown clung to her figure, where she had belted it with the beaded girdle. A white collar set off the golden skin of her face and neck. Her hair was brushed out to dry and it framed her face. She walked awkwardly in the round-toed shoes.

The housekeeper looked at her, with head tilted to one

side. "Just think, I had to get shoes from my lady to fit her. Now I'll get some food to stay her stomach until dinner."

After the boys bathed, John showed Nemud how to use buttons and buckles. "You look funny, Cheegut. Now I know why you want to stay with red men. These long skins make my legs itch and I can't wear the hard boxes. Will the wonnux be angry if I go barefooted?"

"The white people will understand. Just watch and try to do as you see them do. I think they'll cut my hair."

"Will they make you look like a sanop?" Nemud asked.

"No. It will be short, but not shaved. There won't be any crest. They say it's not good for a man to have long hair like a woman. They don't like fancy clothes, either."

"If they had any more things on their bodies they would smother. Let us sit in the sun. We can rest until these strange people do something more to us."

Dinner that night was a new experience for John and his Indian family. The fading light that came through the diamond panes had little effect on the shadows of the room. Tapers flickered in silver or pewter candlesticks. Their light was reflected from the polished walnut table.

The governor seated Wegun at his right and the two boys at the left. Mistress Winthrop was at the foot of the table. Winthrop said grace, which sounded to John like a very long prayer. Nemud held his head bowed, as he saw his foster brother do, but his black eyes were looking in every direction to see what was going to happen next.

John had cautioned Nemud about eating with his fingers. "Watch the governor and do what he does. Be sure to use the same tools he uses when he eats," John said. The dinner proceeded with few mishaps.

There had been little conversation. A servant came in to remove the roast. He whispered something to Winthrop, who smiled and nodded to the man. He turned to John and said, "I shall have to talk to your good foster mother through you. First tell her how pleased we are to have her company."

"I am happy to find white people as good as my Cheegut. Now I am sure my husband was right when he opposed the war against the English," said Wegun.

John translated, leaving out reference to himself.

"Now tell her this. My servant brought me the message that Uncas captured Mononotto. He was wounded, but not seriously. He is now with the Narragansetts. I sent word that he was to be freed and he is to join his wife and son there at Canonicus's fort."

Wegun looked up when she heard the name of her husband. When John translated she moved as if she were going to go to the governor. Then she controlled herself and said to John, "Tell the good man that he has done more than save my life. He has given me back my family."

"And you, young man. You will stay with us," the governor said.

"Isn't it possible for me to stay with Wegun?" John said.

"It is not well for a white boy to live as an Indian. I have a worthy friend in Roxbury who has asked me to let you live with his family. He is a teacher who works with the Indians. He feels that you can help him. You can see your friends from time to time."

Wegun had been watching. When John told her what the governor had said, she nodded. "You are a white boy. It is right that you grow up to do the things you have always wished to do. You have felt that it was your duty, now that duty has been made easy for you. Remember you will always be welcome in the lodge of Mononotto and Wegun."

The next day Wegun and Nemud prepared to leave. John went with them to the town wharf where a shallop was being loaded.

Men were stowing bales and casks in the open boat, while sailors prepared to hoist the sails. "I'll take care of the Injuns, Your Excellency. I'll put them ashore at the Narragansett landing on my way to Aquidneck," the trader said.

John helped Wegun into the boat. Then he stood on the rough planks and tried to keep his lips from trembling.

The vessel moved out slowly, then gathered speed as the sail swelled in the breeze. John watched, but knew that they would not look back. He choked back a sob as the sailboat went out of sight around the point.

Then he turned and took his place beside Governor Winthrop.

GLOSSARY OF
PEQUOT INDIAN WORDS

To Roger Williams I am indebted for the meanings of many of the words used by the Pequots. His *A Key to the Language of America* gives a working knowledge of the speech used by most of the New England red men.

The following words are used in the story:

Abnaki	Indian tribe in northern New England. Name means "much fish."
ahupanum	come here
aque	hello
Aquidneck	Indian name for island where Newport, Rhode Island, is located
baduntah	rising (said of the rising sun)
bedunk	bed (borrowed from the English word)
beush!	come!
biangut	blanket (borrowed from the English word)
bopoose	cat (probably borrowed from English "pussy")
bushkeag	gun
bushkeagun	guns
Capawack	Indian name for Martha's Vineyard
cheegut	sea trout
cheephuggey	dreadful, terrible
Cowesets	Indian tribe north of the Narragansetts
debe	devil (borrowed from English word)
debecornug	home of the evil spirit

duksors	rabbit
ewo	he says
ewash	say it
geeshtush	wash yourself
guldooke	good luck. Name was given to tree formation at Weinshauks, where two trees were joined in growing.
Hobbamuck	Indians' evil spirit
kedeliwizi	you are named
Kiehtan	Indians' good spirit
Leni Lenápe	Algonquin tribe near Delaware, sometimes called the Delawares. Name means "The Real People."
Manisses	Block Island
muckachuck	boy
muttoumbe	pack with a head strap or tumpline
Machemoodus	Indian place name for Moodus, Connecticut.
Mohegan	Indian tribe located near Norwich, Connecticut and related to the Pequots. Name means "man eater."
Mohawks	One of the five tribes of the Five Nations or Iroquois
Mystic	Indian place name meaning "great tidal river." Pequot fort was on hill at what is now West Mystic, Connecticut.
Narragansett	Indian tribe on west side of Narragansett Bay in Rhode Island. Name means "strip of land along the water."
nemud	small brother
netop	friend
nichie	brother

Niantics	Indian tribe in Rhode Island, east of Westerly. They were tributary to the Narragansetts.
Ninigret	This was the Niantics' fort. It was located ten miles east of Westerly, Rhode Island.
Nipmucks	Indian tribe north of the Narragansetts in Connecticut and Massachusetts. Tributary to the Narragansetts.
nuppe	water
Ohomowaukee	Indian place name meaning "Owl's Nest." A swamp north of the Pequot forts.
Paugasucks	An Indian tribe east of the Housatonic River in Connecticut, near Bridgeport and Fairfield.
Pequotoog	Indian tribe located near Mystic and Groton, Connecticut. Name means "Destroyers" and has been shortened, by the white men, to Pequot.
powow	medicine man, magician. Sometimes the name is given to an Indian political talk or to witchcraft.
quahaug	hard clams, often called littlenecks
Quinnebaugs	Indian tribe west of the Mohegans and Pequots
Quonnihticut	Indian name for the Connecticut River. The early settlers took many of the Indian names for their rivers and towns. Many of our states have Indian names.
sachem	Indian noble

sanop	Indian brave or warrior
Shawmut	Indian name for Boston
Shawomets	Indian tribe, tributary to the Narragansetts, located at what is now Warren, Rhode Island.
shkook	snake
shquaaw	woman or squaw
succotash	stew of corn and beans with meat or fish
tawhitch kuppeyaumen?	What come you for?
teecommewas	striker—hitter
tulepas	turtle
Unkuowa	Indian name for swamp near Fairfield, Connecticut
Wabaquassets	Indian tribe west of the Mohegans and Pequots
wahsus	bear
Wampanoags	Indian tribe in eastern Massachusetts (Massasoit was sachem)
Wangunks	Indian tribe near Hartford and Wethersfield, on the Connecticut River.
weeqwasun	good morning
wegun	good
wequash	swan
Weinshauks	Indian place name. This was the headquarters and fort of Sassacus, chief sachem of the Pequots.
wenai	old woman
wesassu	he is afraid
wonnux	white man
wunx	fox
yokeg	parched corn